BATTLE FATIGUE

Also by Mark Kurlansky

BATTLE

FATGUE

MARK KURLANSKY

Walker & Company

New York

First published in the United States of America in October 2011
by Walker Publishing Company, Inc., a division of Bloomsbury Publishing, Inc.
www.bloomsburyteens.com

For information about permission to reproduce selections from this book, write to
Permissions, Walker BFYR, 175 Fifth Avenue, New York, New York 10010

Lyrics on page 225 from "I Feel Like I'm Fixin' to Die Rag"; words and music by
Joe McDonald © 1965 Alkatraz Corner Music Co. Used by permission.

Library of Congress Cataloging-in-Publication Data
Kurlansky, Mark.
Battle fatigue / by Mark Kurlansky. — 1st U.S. ed.
p.   cm.
Summary: Joel Bloom chronicles his life experiences during the 1960s which eventually lead him
to oppose the war in Vietnam and to flee to Canada rather than be forced to kill Vietnamese.
ISBN 978-0-8027-2264-5 (hardcover)
1. Vietnam War, 1961–1975—Draft resisters—Juvenile fiction. [1. Vietnam War, 1961–1975—
Draft resisters—Fiction. 2. Draft resisters—Fiction. 3. Friendship—Fiction.] I. Title.
PZ7.K9595Bat 2011   [Fic]—dc22   2011006392

Book design by Regina Roff
Typeset by Westchester Book Composition
Printed in the U.S.A. by Quad/Graphics, Fairfield, Pennsylvania
2 4 6 8 10 9 7 5 3 1

All papers used by Bloomsbury Publishing, Inc., are natural, recyclable products
made from wood grown in well-managed forests. The manufacturing processes
conform to the environmental regulations of the country of origin.

To Talia Feiga, her generation,
and their dream of a better world

If a man does not keep pace with his companions,
perhaps it is because he hears a
different drummer.

—*WALDEN*, HENRY DAVID THOREAU, 1854

PROLOGUE
SNAG IN THE PLAN

It is a cold fall day and I am thinking of Canada—thinking of how cold Canada will be. Everything seems to be going so fast. Only three years ago I was a teenager. Now I am a refugee, a political exile—or I will be soon. After a year and a half of appeals, I'm just waiting for the final decision of my draft board. I know what that decision is going to be. And then I can either go to prison or to Canada. I think Canada would be better, but it is not without its drawbacks.

I have never been to Canada though I was close once. I demonstrated on a bridge right at the border. Maybe it would have been easier if I had just crossed over then and not come back.

I'm sitting in my bedroom in dim bluish New England light, skimming through a booklet with a yellow cover called *Manual for Draft-Age Immigrants to Canada*. I paid two dollars for it. It has a lot of information about how to go to Canada as a draft resister and get legal status. The book was put together by people who want us to refuse to fight and to come to Canada, so it tries to be reassuring. It has a chapter titled "Yes, John, There Is a Canada." The next chapter is "It Has Politics," and it explains which political parties oppose the war. The next chapter asserts that Canada does have a culture, followed by a chapter claiming that Canada has real cities. And then, finally, the book gets to the real point—Canada has snow.

The temperature in Canada is very much on my mind. The town that I come from in eastern Massachusetts, Haley, was named after Martin Haley, who fought and died in Canada in the mid-1700s in the French and Indian War. He was my age when he died but he got a town named after him, and I suppose he was the original reason that being a war hero was considered so important in Haley. When we were little we used to hear, and often made up, stories about how many Indians Martin Haley had killed—or was it Frenchmen he killed?—before they got him. We weren't sure, but he must have killed a lot of some kind of people to have a town named after him.

But when we got a little older we heard the story that it wasn't Indians or Frenchmen that killed him. It was Canada. He went up to Canada and it was so cold that he got sick and died. All the kids thought this was a great joke and we used to play Martin Haley Goes to War, which consisted of a bugle call, the drawing of a sword, a sneeze, and then someone falling over. We would all laugh.

This remains my image of Canada. The *Manual for Draft-Age Immigrants to Canada* states that a temperature of eighty-one degrees below zero had once been recorded in a town called Snag. I am not going to move to Snag. The booklet says the temperature in Toronto averages seventy-one in July. But it also says Toronto gets fifty-five inches of snow a year. Is the best that can be said of Toronto that it is better than Snag?

I have settled on Vancouver, which only gets twenty-four inches of snow. The manual also says that chocolate chip cookies cost forty-nine cents a pound in Vancouver, while they cost fifty-seven cents a pound in Toronto. It does not give cookie prices in Snag.

This is how I am making decisions these days. I'll take the town with the least snow and the cheapest cookies. After having made the one big decision that I have spent my whole life thinking about, all the rest are now tossed out on things like the price of cookies.

How did it come to this? How did I, Joel Bloom, become a political exile? I had always thought I was a fairly normal American kid. Maybe a little different, but I loved baseball. In fact, I am still excited about the 1971 World Series. Baltimore, with one of the best pitching staffs in history, is taking on the Pittsburgh Pirates with Roberto Clemente. This could be one of the great seven-game series.

My only problem is that I don't want to kill Vietnamese people. Like Martin Haley, I turn out not to be an Indian slayer. That has disappointed a lot of people. I have always known that I would have to face war and I have always thought about it. Even as a small child in Haley I could see it coming. But back then I mostly wondered how I would do. I didn't know that there was a choice, a decision to be made. It has taken me all these years to make it, but looking back I see how most everything in my life—even things that didn't seem very important at the time—was leading to this decision. Only when I look back at all of it do I really understand what happened.

PART ONE
MY CHILDHOOD

CHAPTER ONE
DOING THE GREAT THING

I know that because I am a boy I will go to war. Boys in Haley go to war. I don't know who I am going to fight. Possibly the Germans or the Russians. It will come, probably when I turn eighteen. I am only seven now so I have a lot of time. I'm not worried. It's just what happens.

All the buildings in Haley are brick. In the summer the bricks look a reddish-chocolate color. It is easy to imagine that the whole town is made of chocolate, everyone living in little chocolate houses and going to the chocolate school. The town looks a little prettier in the summer when it becomes green. There are a lot of very big maple trees, which are the best trees for climbing because the branches start low to the ground. We sometimes split the wing-shaped sticky green seeds and put them on our noses so we look like long-nosed Martians. Maybe we will end up fighting Martians—with ray guns. I have a toy ray gun.

In the winter, with no leaves and cold light, the bricks turn blackish, the town looks hard, and there is no dreaming it away. It is a hard town of brick factories that produce small hard things like tools and metal wire and ball bearings that make engines turn. Sometimes we play with ball bearings—shoot them like silvery marbles. I am not sure how they make machines run but that is what they say.

Just before I was born there was the Big War, the biggest war ever, World War II. Everyone fought it, all over the world. I know this because all the men in town ask each other where they were during the war, and the answers are strange names from far away. But when the war was over the soldiers came to Haley because Haley had jobs. Everyone has a job in Haley, most of them in the factories.

My father went to war, my uncle went to war, the fathers of everyone I know went to war, every man in the neighborhood went. Then they came home and had all of us.

My father was in the Pacific, which, I have learned, is the world's largest ocean. He was an officer, which is a good thing to be. I think I would like to be an officer but it must be a hard thing to get because none of the other dads were officers. They were privates and corporals and sergeants. But once you become an officer, you can become a general. For some reason, though, my dad didn't like it very much. He doesn't like to talk about it. I have never seen a picture of him in his officer uniform but I'm sure he must have looked fantastic. That is one of the things about being an officer. You get much better uniforms. All the other kids have pictures of their fathers in plain uniforms set out in their living rooms. But there is no picture of my father in his officer uniform.

I went with him once to a clothing store. He was looking for a raincoat. He searched through a long line of them, shoving them over one by one like he was hitting them.

A salesman came over looking unhappy. I thought he was going to tell my father not to hit the raincoats but all he said was, "Can I help you, sir?"

"Yes, don't you have any coats without these damn epaulets?" My father slapped the coats one more time. He was going to get into trouble.

"I'll go and look," was all the salesman said, and then he left.

"Dad?" I said.

He didn't answer. He was staring at the raincoats.

"Dad?" I repeated.

"Yes," he said, shaking his head and changing his tone of voice as if he had just been awakened from a spell. "What is it?"

"Dad? What's an epaulet?"

"It's this," he said, poking at a raincoat. A strip of cloth was stuck to the coat near the collar and it buttoned on the other end, at the shoulder. "When I was in the army, everything I wore had these things on it. Well, I don't have to wear them anymore," he said angrily.

I wonder what he did in the war. I know he was in New Guinea, though I am not sure where that is. We have a painting hanging in the living room. A green and red jungle. I always thought it was a painting of where he had been in New Guinea, but I was wrong. It is a copy of a painting I found by accident in a book. It is by a famous French artist named Paul Gauguin. The book said it is a painting of Tahiti, which my mother showed me on a map. It is not even near New Guinea. The Pacific is very big.

I can feel New Guinea in our home, and so I am always looking for signs of it. There is a black stone ax with straw in the center—an odd-shaped thing—hanging on the wall. And this really is from New Guinea. It belonged to a kind of Indian in the Pacific. It was his tool—or was it a weapon?

I often stare up at the strange T-shaped object, trying to decide.

"Stay away from that thing, Joel," my mother says. "If that thing falls down it will split your head in two."

It seems to me that everything is more—just more—in our house. Other kids are told to be careful with things because they could "put an eye out." But in our house you could split your head in two, which seems even harder to fix. I avoid the wall with the ax.

Another thing my father brought back from New Guinea is even scarier. It is called malaria, and it causes sweat to pour out of him—like juices are being squeezed out by something crushing him. He shakes so hard that it seems he might come apart. You can talk to him while he sits there shaking. I like to because it proves to me that he will be all right. There are fewer attacks than before and they are not as bad. The war seems to be wearing off.

My uncle is very different. He was not an officer and he didn't fight in the Pacific. He fought the Germans in Europe and he does talk about it. He seems to have been everywhere in Europe inside a tank. I don't think you can see much from inside a tank because he cannot describe anything, only an endless list of places he has been—Normandy, Paris, Bastogne, the Rhine, the Elbe . . . The French have a drink called Calvados, which he said was very nice and very strong and got him very drunk, and the Belgians had cherry-flavored beer, and the Russians had tea that was so strong it was black and tasted like coffee.

But there is something missing from his war stories. There is never any mention of fighting—only the places and the drinks. Sometimes, when my uncle is babysitting at night, I go into the living room to watch television and I turn on the lamp. My uncle is right there, sitting in a chair, silent, his light-gray eyes wide open. Without turning or moving he says in a very low soft voice, "Hello."

He spends a lot of time on that one chair with its white cover printed with designs of roses and lots of leaves, just sitting there in the dark.

I go to the television and turn the dial. There are five stations. At least one of them will have something about the war—old news films or a television program or even a movie. Movies about World War II are everywhere. They are about the men. There is always a farm boy who knew nothing and there is always a kid from Brooklyn who knows too much and is not completely honest. And there is usually an Italian and a Jew and a Pole, which is pretty much what our neighborhood is like too. These men would become friends from fighting together, killing the enemy, and sometimes getting killed—but in the end becoming *men*, doing what men have to do. War is how you grow and become a man.

My uncle always asks me to stop on the war movie and usually it is about his war. When the film gives the name of a place, he says, in a low voice with no emotion that I can hear, "I was there." Sometimes when they mention a place— "We're going to Bastogne"—he will repeat the name. "Bastogne," he will say, making a sound with his mouth like he needs to let some air out.

When the movie is over he stops talking. I turn off the television and he does not move—doesn't even turn his head. I don't think his eyes are moving.

"Well, I guess I'll go to bed," I say, and I don't wait for him to answer.

As I walk out of the room, he asks me to turn the light off, and I leave him staring into the dark as if he has his own television to watch when the real one is off. He is back in his war.

I do know a little about my uncle's war from my mother. My mother has not been to war and so is more willing to talk about it. My uncle was in something called the Battle of the Bulge and then he fought across Germany. His group met the Russians, who were fighting across Germany from the other side, at a river. According to my mother, he also helped capture a concentration camp called Dachau.

I know what a concentration camp is because my grandfather's family disappeared in one and my grandfather has been writing a lot of letters to the Red Cross trying to find them. These camps were places where Germans held Jews and every day sent some away to be killed. I don't know why they would do this and my uncle never says anything about these places. Neither does my grandfather.

Every Friday morning I go with my mother to the bakery to get a challah and an onion rye bread, hot out of the oven. Onion rye bread hot out of the oven is one of the best things about my childhood. I would like to eat an entire loaf, steamy and bitter and sour and even sweet, with its hard crust and soft silvery middle—just breaking it apart with my hands. No butter or slicing or anything. But this is something I never get to do.

My mother orders the bread and a woman with her dark hair in a scarf, wearing a white coat, takes this soft and heavy loaf and slides it into a white paper bag and hands it over the counter to me. She always hands it to me, not my mother and, as she reaches down, the white sleeve of her coat slides up her wrist and I can see the blue numbers, a long row of them, on her arm. I can never look into her eyes because I know those eyes have seen terrible things and it scares me.

I will admit that I am afraid of concentration camps. My parents said that millions, including my grandfather's brothers and sisters and parents, were murdered in them by poison. My parents and other grown-ups argue about how much I should be told about this and that makes me listen carefully. So now I have found out everything. The Nazis poisoned people in showers and made lamp shades and bars of soap from Jewish people. This was how I learned that grown-ups do things that are stranger than anything kids can think up. We once played a game where if you were captured you were turned into spaghetti and then you couldn't stand up. But this was even stranger. This was the worst thing. My uncle had done a great thing by capturing the concentration camp and killing the Germans or putting them in jail or whatever he did. That is the part no one will tell me about.

✗ ✗ ✗

All of my grandparents were born in Europe somewhere. They never explain where. Sometimes I hear my mother's father speaking Polish with the Polish people in town.

"So Grandpa," I say. "You speak Polish?"

"Echhh," he says, rotating his hands palm up and then palm down to indicate "maybe, maybe not."

"So you're from Poland?"

"Echhh."

He never explains.

"They all had terrible lives in Europe," my mother says.

"Why was it terrible?" I ask.

"The Poles hated the Jews. They rode through the towns on horseback beating people and killing them and setting houses on fire."

I tried to imagine this. The only thing I had ever seen that sounded anything like this was something I once saw on television about people covered with sheets who rode through a town setting things on fire. They were called the Ku Klux Klan.

"Was it like the Ku Klux Klan?" I ask.

"Something like that," she says. "And we would have all lived like that if my parents hadn't gotten us out. Then it got even worse."

"The concentration camp."

"Yes," she says. "You know about that, Joel?" Why wouldn't I know about that? The grown-ups talk about it every day. "But they got out, walking all the way to Hamburg."

"And that's why we were not in the concentration camp?"

"Yes," she says.

✖ ✖ ✖

So I understand that fighting for America is a very good thing. My father did a good thing fighting the Japanese because they attacked America in Pearl Harbor and so

America made them pay, dropping atomic bombs on them. It was a good thing. My uncle killed the Germans who wanted to poison people in the shower. That was a good thing too. All the men in my neighborhood had done great things and someday I would be called on to do a great thing.

CHAPTER TWO

THE RIGHT WAY TO PLAY WAR

I owe my popularity to a Nazi sign—my parents call it a "swastika." I don't know what this word means but it is a bent and broken cross that stands for the Nazis who ran concentration camps—I have some. We all play war and we have good things for playing it because our fathers brought home great stuff from the real war. We have brown-green uniforms, field jackets with instructions printed inside by the U.S. Army on how to stay warm and dry while fighting. Mine is very baggy and goes down to my feet but it is a real combat jacket, which my uncle calls "combat fatigues."

I also have a wool jacket, called an Eisenhower jacket, which has shoulder pads that make me look big and soldier-like. Maybe that was why Eisenhower liked it too. Eisenhower was a general, so this must have been an officer's uniform, which is why it looks so good.

A bunch of us have German helmets. But I have something even better—two gray fur hats with Nazi swastikas on the front. And two canteens with the same signs. Kids in the neighborhood want to play war with me because I have the hats and canteens.

Dickey Panicelli has the best thing. He always has the coolest everything. His father is a policeman and carries a gun and is the only person, aside from the woman at the bakery, I ever saw with a tattoo. He was in the navy and has an anchor on his forearm, which makes him look like Popeye in the cartoons. We all call him Popeye and he doesn't seem to mind.

Popeye Panicelli brought back from his war a big white Japanese flag with a large red dot in the center. He also has a Japanese sword but we are not allowed to play with it. Popeye showed it to me once. He took it out of its case and waved a piece of paper across the blade and the paper was cut in two. That's how sharp it is. The Japanese used these swords to chop off their own heads rather than surrender. That's what Popeye says, but then he starts staring past the sword, that same stare that my uncle has, and he doesn't say anything for a minute.

"Dad!" says Dickey. Popeye looks at him and then he is okay and smiles and starts putting the sword away. So I decide to bring Dickey over to my uncle's house to show what I have—also something we are not allowed to take outside—a German rifle. It is dark wood and the metal part where you put the bullet has a black rod that slides in and out. I like the feel of it, pulling the heavy rod out and up by a handle, pretending to slip in a round, slapping the handle down, and jamming it in. Ready for combat. The only problem is that to do this you have to hold the gun with one hand, and it is so heavy I can barely lift it with both arms. I have to rest the whole thing on my lap to play with the bolt. My brother and I have contests to see who can hold the rifle straight out and for how long. But neither of us can hold it up for more than a second or two. I can do a little better than he can.

When we play war, Dickey doesn't join us because he is three years older. But he lets us use his Japanese flag to surrender.

He is always busy building things with lawn mower engines. Where does he get all the lawn mowers? He builds metal frames that he says are made out of beds. Whose beds? Then he puts the engine on the frame and adds wheels and he has a cart with a very loud motor that he can drive around the neighborhood. His white T-shirts always have grease on them.

In our wars there are rules. The Germans can't surrender. The Germans always have to die. But the Japanese surrender. I'm not sure why. Maybe because we have a Japanese flag and we don't have a German one, so the Germans don't have anything to surrender with. I wonder, though, shouldn't the Japanese be chopping their heads off? But in our wars they just surrender. They did surrender in the real war too. Whatever the reason, you would think this makes playing a German a bad deal. Still, you would be surprised how many kids want to be Germans. In fact, everyone wants to be a German because you get to wear one of the hats or one of the helmets or carry a canteen. If you are Japanese all you have is a flag for surrendering. My brother likes being a German and wearing one of the fur hats and I enjoy being the American who kills him. I get to kill him in several different ways on a good summer afternoon.

"*Tdg-tdg-tdg-kadush*," I say, pointing my toy wooden Western rifle that doubles as a machine gun. And my brother jerks several times and spins and then falls dead, being careful not to let the fur cap fall on the ground. Sometimes he places the cap over his face as he lays dead. Or I jump on him and stab him with my make-believe knife. I can do whatever I want because he is the German and I am the American and the Americans always win and the Germans die. After he dies I take his hat to bring home to my family in America as a souvenir. He is happy that he gets to play with us.

I am two years older than my brother, Sam, and I have always been glad that I was born first because, even though he is already as big as me, being born first gives me the advantage in most things. I even have a better birthday: I was born on December 7, on the seventh anniversary of the bombing of Pearl Harbor. Your birthday is always the most exciting day of the year. But on my special day everybody talks about the bombing of Pearl Harbor, "the sneak attack," and what they were doing when they found out.

"I was making lasagna," Popeye Panicelli's wife says, emphasizing the word "lasagna" as though it were a clue to understanding World War II—and maybe it is.

"We were planning our first car trip," says my father.

On my birthday, newspapers write about Pearl Harbor and it is talked about on television.

"Look at this, will ya," says my uncle, and I walk over. There on the television screen are films of ships sinking with black smoke coming out of them.

"Wow!" I say.

"Look at her go," says my uncle. There is a long pause

and then he adds, "The old *Arizona*." Another long pause. "There she goes." And a minute later, "Look at her go."

My birthday is the same every year. The same pictures on television, my uncle saying the same things with the same pauses. Even during the rest of the year, after I tell people when my birthday is, they start talking about it. "What day is your birthday, Joel?" asked Stanley Wiszcinski's mom in April when I was at the Wiszcinskis' house for Stanley's birthday.

"December seventh," I answered, and just waited for the response.

"December seventh! Who will ever forget that day? I was knitting a sweater when I heard."

I smiled and nodded politely. Grown-ups are so excited to talk about this that I am never sure if it is supposed to be the worst or the best day of their lives.

My brother, on the other hand, was born on January 3. People don't remember what they were doing that day, except my uncle. He could celebrate Sam's birthday too.

"January third," he says. "We were given extra rounds and we moved up."

"Moved up where?" my brother asks. I already know the answer.

"The Ardennes forest, Ardennes, the forest . . ." He gets lost in thought. January 3 is the anniversary of when the Allies broke through the German lines. I don't really know what that means but breaking through seems to be big. It was the Bulge, which seems a weird name for a battle. My uncle was there.

For a long time I thought people could just arrange to have their kids on the anniversaries of important battles and that when I was ready to have children they would be born on the anniversaries of battles that have not yet been fought but that would be important to me. In time I came to realize—and Sam did too—that his birthday was not as important as mine, except maybe to my uncle. But I don't care about Sam feeling bad about not having as good a date as me, so I just dress him up as a German and tell him it is the Bulge and kill him.

When Tony Scaratini comes over he insists on being a German too. Tony is the neighborhood bully. He is bigger than the rest of us and we are all a little afraid of him.

"I'm the German. Give me the hat," he demands.

"We already have the Germans picked out," I say.

Tony twists his face. He has a way of twisting it that makes him look really mean. Also very ugly. "You know why I'm the German?" he says in a menacing tone as he looks down at me.

I do know why—because he is going to beat me up if I don't let him be the German. But he wants to explain anyway. "I'm Italian!" he announces.

Now I am getting curious. "So? You're Italian?"

"The Italians were on the side with the Germans. And we don't have any real Germans here, right? So I should get to be the German. I'm as close as you got!"

I hand him the hat, relieved to have an excuse to give it to him without fighting about it, even though I hate the way he plays a German. He plays like he expects the Germans to win.

Donnie LePine always plays an American. There is never any debate about that because, obviously, Donnie LePine is going to win. He wins at everything and always does everything well, and he is more popular than me even though he doesn't have any World War II hats or things. His father was a navy officer in the Pacific but he didn't bring anything good back. Donnie doesn't need it. The other kids look up to me just because Donnie LePine is willing to come over to my place to play. I would like to get to kill him, or at least make him surrender, but he is an American and will never know defeat. Side by side we liberate Europe and the Pacific.

"*Tdg-tdg-tdg-kadush-kadush.*" I charge the Germans, my brother and Tony, from across the backyard, fighting next to Donnie LePine, who is firing: "*Gudj. Gudj-gudj.*" He also brings in an artillery barrage: "*Whaaaaa-k'brrm!*" That was his little thing. I never heard the phrase "barrage" before.

The Germans are holding their own. "*Dew-dew-whack

dew." But finally we get up there and I knock my brother down, pretend, with the rifle butt and then shoot him while he clutches his hat.

But Tony is always a problem. Finally Donnie says, "Tony, you're dead. You have to lie down."

"I'm not dead, Donnie."

"You wanted to be a German. The Germans die," Donnie insists.

"Okay, I'm surrendering."

"You can't surrender. You're a German."

"All right," Tony says, and he just leaves the yard and walks home.

"Tony!" I shout. "My hat. You can't take my hat!"

But he just keeps walking. I have to have my parents get it from his parents, which is embarrassing. But that is what Tony is like.

"I got da hat," says Donnie in a perfect Scaratini voice. We all do Scaratini but only Donnie does it well. Donnie has a perfect voice and when we have to sing in school he is the one the teachers pay attention to. Tony has a voice like a cough. But Donnie does it best and we all laugh and try to do it too: "I got da hat." We all laugh, but I'm the one who has to tell my parents.

Stanley Wiszcinski is the smallest kid in the neighborhood, so we make him play the Japanese and surrender in a serious ceremony in which he turns over the flag. Then we push him around a little for bombing Pearl Harbor, but also because everyone likes to pick on Stanley.

Rocco Pizzutti doesn't play war. Rocco is a perfect cube—as wide and thick as he is tall—with one thick black eyebrow that goes all the way across the top of his face, marking it like a Hebrew vowel. Rocco never says very much and he looks at his sister, Angela, in a way that makes everyone afraid to talk to her, which is too bad because she is the only girl I know that you could actually call pretty. Lucky for her, she didn't get the eyebrow.

Rocco and his sister do not have a father because their father was killed in what we always call "the Korean conflict." It is never called a war and when I ask my mother why not, she explains that it wasn't a war, it was "a police action." I don't understand what a police action is but I know it was bad enough for Rocco and Angela Pizzutti's father to die. If asked about their father, they don't get upset but they always say, "He was killed in the Korean War."

They are the only ones who call it a war.

Sometimes, if my brother complains about being made to play a German all the time, I tell him to be quiet or I will make him play a Korean. Then he would still die, but it wouldn't even be a real war. That usually makes him be quiet.

✗ ✗ ✗

Bernie, the vegetable man, is making a delivery while we are playing and we attack him with our toy guns, our helmets and hats, and our flag. Bernie Vegetable—that's what we call him—starts sweating, and his hands, holding fruit, start to shake. He picks up a squash and shakes it like it is a musical instrument. But he isn't joking around.

Bernie was a marine in the Pacific and maybe he has the same thing as my dad had. We don't know that much about him. There is a teacher in school who was in Europe and if you drop your books really loudly, he jumps and shakes and sweats. Kids slam things on purpose to see if they can get him to shake. His name is Mr. Schacter but we all call him Mr. Shaker. He teaches older kids and we are very glad that it will be a lot more years before we have to have Mr. Shaker for a teacher. Maybe Mr. Shaker and Bernie Vegetable have the same thing. I heard my father call it "battle fatigue." Is that like my jacket that is called "fatigues"? Does wearing the jacket make you that way or are they called "fatigues" because people wearing fatigues often get fatigue? I don't know.

CHAPTER THREE
THE CHAMPIONS

Now that I am almost eight years old, I feel I am old enough to take a stand on things. I may try to do this more often, but for now it is simply this: the New York Yankees must go down in defeat. Now and always.

The Brooklyn Dodgers are the team of the people. They are the team of the civil rights movement. They have integrated baseball, with Jackie Robinson and Roy Campanella. In the South, Martin Luther King and the Freedom Riders are jailed, beaten, and pushed off the street by the rush of water from big hoses. I see it on television. In Brooklyn the Dodgers are playing and winning. So the line is clearly drawn: Dodgers or Yankees. Civil rights or not. Most of the other kids don't care because they are Red Sox fans. I am not sure about the Red Sox, but I like teams that take on the Yankees so I guess I am okay with the Red Sox winning.

I have not been a Dodgers fan for long. This, in fact, is the first year I have followed baseball at all. The Dodgers are the defending champions. Donnie LePine keeps saying that the year before was the first year they ever won. But there is no reason to believe him. He is a Yankees fan, and doesn't that just figure. The whole reason I got interested in baseball this year is that the evil Yankees are trying to unseat the champions. The Dodgers struggled all summer, whereas the Yankees had an easy season. People like Donnie, who don't understand struggling, root for the Yankees. Donnie never struggles. That's why he likes the Yankees. Also, the Yankees wear stupid striped uniforms that look like the kind of pajamas I always hate wearing.

Nobody else in school or in the neighborhood seems to be rooting for the Dodgers. Mr. Shaker even put up a Yankees banner in his classroom, dramatically tacking it on the wall like he was planting a flag. One day it fell down, making a flopping noise behind him and Mr. Shaker dropped his head as though ducking for cover. All the kids saw him do it and they laughed and it was talked about all over school.

They are all Red Sox fans but since the series has come

down to the Dodgers and the Yankees, they are leaning toward the Yankees—even though they are supposed to hate them. They are Yankees fans just like they support Eisenhower against Adlai Stevenson. Adlai Stevenson seems like a nice man but, after all, Eisenhower won the war. Popeye Panicelli even says, or so Dickey told us, that Stevenson was a traitor to be running against Eisenhower. "You don't run against the General," he says. "It's not American."

Most everyone feels that way—except my uncle, who served under Eisenhower when he won the war. He hates the General.

"I've got no use for that guy," he says.

"Wasn't he your commander?" I ask.

"Just no use for him."

"Why?"

There is no answer.

It is hard to find a Stevenson supporter or a Brooklyn fan. Going into the third game of the World Series, I seem to be the only happy kid in Haley. Brooklyn won the first two games. In the second they beat up the Yankees pitcher, a not-very-good pitcher named Don Larsen, who does not even have a windup before he throws—the kind of loser the Yankees deserve. They had to take him out of the game in the second inning.

But the Yankees win the third game with their star pitcher, Whitey Ford.

"Here they come," says a happy Donnie LePine. He is wearing a blue Yankees hat that his father bought him over the summer when they went to Yankee Stadium. He also has a ball, which he says he caught from a home run off Mickey Mantle's bat. He may have been lying but Donnie LePine is lucky enough that it could be true. He let us all touch the ball but he would never play with it.

"Joel, it's over for your guys," Donnie says.

"The Dodgers are the champions," I insist.

"Not for long."

I am not worried. Then the Yankees win the fourth game and the series is tied.

But my father, who may be quietly rooting for the Dodgers—I think he may just as quietly be voting for Stevenson—tells me not to worry about game five. Sal Maglie, who destroyed Whitey Ford in game one, is pitching. He is the toughest man in baseball, mean-looking and never clean shaven. He looks a bit like Rocco Pizzutti and smiles about that much too. The best the Yankees can do is put in Don Larsen, who had been taken out in the second inning of game two. Even Yankees fans call Larsen "Gooney Bird."

"Are you ready for Gooney Bird?" I tease Donnie. He doesn't answer.

✕ ✕ ✕

Maglie is pitching beautifully, as I knew he would. But so is Gooney Bird. No one is hitting. Then in the fourth inning Mickey Mantle hits a home run. But I am not worried because the Brooklyn Dodgers have Jackie Robinson, Roy Campanella, Gil Hodges, and Duke Snider, and they are only one run behind.

But now the radio announcer is saying unbelievable things. They have all struck out. Come on! Over and over again. No hits, no walks, no errors—the perfect game. And that cements my hatred of the New York Yankees—and my love of baseball.

✗ ✗ ✗

The Dodgers have their revenge. The next game has no score and is in extra innings. All of a sudden Jackie Robinson drives in a run and wins the game for Brooklyn! I don't have to say anything to Donnie LePine—I just smile and enjoy it.

✗ ✗ ✗

It is the last game and the Yankees win 9–0, taking the World Series. Eisenhower has won by a similar score. These things go together—the Yankees, the Republican Party, Donnie LePine.

I understand that we live in Massachusetts and so people root for the Red Sox. But why would anyone root for the Yankees? Or vote for Eisenhower? Those people are just like that and there isn't much that can be done about it.

I learn a lot from baseball.

CHAPTER FOUR
WHEN GROWN-UPS START CRYING

Now that I am eleven years old, practically a teenager, we don't play war anymore. Instead we play baseball. I am a center fielder with a good throwing arm, though not as good a range for fielding as I should have. I hit pretty well, which makes up for what a bad base runner I am. Unfortunately my competition for center field is Tony Scaratini, the bad German, who gets not only larger every year but also meaner. No one really likes him but no one is going to tell him. Donnie LePine still does the best Scaratini imitation, and that is as close as anyone comes to telling him off. Tony runs bases as badly as me and he can't field at all. When a fly ball goes to center field he just stands there. If the ball comes right at him he will raise his glove. Otherwise, his feeling is that it is someone else's problem. He is the kind of player coaches don't like. Except that he can hit a ball clean out of the park. "There!" he barks, forgetting to run in case the ball doesn't leave the park. But it is usually gone.

"There!" Donnie barks just like him, and we all laugh, all trying to say it like Tony too, but only Donnie has it right. Tony is going to kill him someday. Except that Tony seems almost afraid of Donnie. If you look closely at Tony, you can see a lot of fear. But he is large.

Stanley Wiszcinski is no longer surrendering. He is managing the team and he is great at it. He always has the batter's box and the baselines perfectly limed, the bats and balls lined up, and even gum for us to chew—striped gum, each color a different flavor. It is one of those special things you get for being a baseball player.

Rocco Pizzutti is our left-handed third baseman. When he catches the ball, everyone runs for cover. He fires it so hard out of his left hand that it hurts to catch it. Sometimes it goes to first base where the play is, but often he misses and hits the pitcher in the back or gets closer to second base.

One afternoon we are playing a good hitting team. The first batter hits a grounder to third base and Rocco fires it to first. The first baseman gets it in his glove but then drops it, shaking his hand in pain. The next batter hits another grounder to Rocco and this time he fires it at the lead runner at second base. The second baseman, Brian Sorenstag, never wants to catch a throw from Rocco. He's already caught a few and it always hurts. Now he just gets out of the way. He is saving his hands for basketball. This means that the runner will be safe on second base or, worse, that Rocco has thrown so hard the ball will end up in the outfield and the runner gets to third. So I run in to catch the throw from Rocco that Brian did not want to touch. Then I understand why. The pain in my hand is so sharp I completely forget about tossing the ball to second.

Of course, our best player is Donnie LePine at shortstop. He never makes fielding errors, his throws are always on target, sometimes he goes to the mound and pitches a few innings, and he has a perfect swing without ever taking batting practice. What makes this even worse, everybody likes him best.

Even the coach, Mr. Bradley, likes LePine best. You can tell. He tries to let everyone play, so players are constantly being taken out. Only Donnie LePine plays all nine innings of every game.

Mr. Bradley is interesting to me. For one thing, he knows absolutely everything about baseball. If you talk about Sal

Maglie, he will tell you his earned run average. Mr. Bradley used to be a pitcher and knows everything about all the pitchers. He is younger than the other teachers and one of the few adult men I know who has never been to war. He has never even been in the military.

All his scars are from baseball and he has quite a few. He was a pitcher for the Pawtucket Red Sox in Rhode Island but "threw his arm out." That is the phrase everyone uses and whatever it means, it must have hurt. One day in the locker room I see his right shoulder. It is misshapen, with a strange dent in the middle covered with long whitish scars. "Oh, my God," I think with horror. "That's what it means—you literally throw your arm out of your body. Then they have to stick it back somehow." I keep thinking about that scarred-up shoulder.

The revenge for the 1956 World Series finally comes. It is four years later and there aren't any Brooklyn Dodgers anymore. This year the Yankees and the Republicans lose, both in very close contests. The World Series comes down to the last inning of the last game, the Pittsburgh Pirates and the Yankees tied. Suddenly a Pittsburgh batter I'd never heard of and who is not known to be much of a hitter smashes the ball out of the park. It is reported that Mickey Mantle cried.

Mickey Mantle cried! I love that. I will always like the

Pirates for that, the team that made Mickey Mantle cry. Adults don't cry very much. The only crying adults I have seen were my family one Saturday when they were listening to a broadcast of *Tosca* with Leontyne Price. It was my parents' favorite opera. I didn't really understand it but it seemed to involve love and torture, and the performers sung these amazing songs with so much feeling. After one song I looked over at my parents and their eyes were shining. They had been crying. Leontyne Price had made them cry. And now the Pittsburgh Pirates had made Mickey Mantle cry. When adults start crying, it's usually important.

CHAPTER FIVE
PAYING THE PRICE

The big thing is that John Kennedy has been elected president. You may not think this is such a big thing. But I've just turned twelve years old and the only president I can remember is Eisenhower. It seemed like he always had been president and always would be president. He was the General, the one who had led all our fathers to war, and had won the war, and so he would be president forever. He was old and he talked the way old people talk, like from a different time. He was all about a world that happened before I was born.

Now he is gone. We all knew Richard Nixon, who ran against Kennedy. If Nixon had won it would not have been exciting because he was Eisenhower's vice president. Like Eisenhower, he had always been there. Also, adults could argue about Nixon, but kids looked into his eyes and didn't trust him. He was scary-looking.

But Kennedy is different. He is young. Everybody says he is young, although actually he isn't. He is the exact same age as my father and no one is calling my father young. But Kennedy is a lot younger than presidents usually are— in other words, a lot younger than Eisenhower. And his wife, Jackie, is amazing. Who could have imagined such a thing, someone that beautiful living in the White House? Everything will be different now. Everything will be young, beautiful, and exciting.

✕ ✕ ✕

To lead us through this time in history, we have our civics teacher, Mr. Walter. I can't figure out what civics is— something about learning to be good citizens. This year it is all about the election.

Every now and then teachers turn up who don't seem like one of the rest of them. It is always surprising that they got their jobs. These teachers are the only ones we ever listen to. Mr. Walter is one of them. He wears his hair a little too long so that it flops in front of his face when he becomes excited—like when he talks about Kennedy and turns to the class and says, "Man, can you dig it?" It really is a question. He wants to know if we are digging it. He plays a wailing alto sax whenever he is left alone. We can hear him playing alone in the classroom after school. Mr. Walter is a beatnik. Beatniks have long hair and listen to wild music and like crazy paintings and poems that don't rhyme. They aren't new anymore. They were new when I was little. But I only know that from television. Mr. Walter is the first beatnik anyone has seen in Haley. In Haley, long hair, especially with curls in the front, is seen on boys who are always in trouble. So this is all very surprising for a teacher.

Mr. Walter wants us to listen to President Kennedy's inaugural address. He has a copy and he reads it in class even though he doesn't have Kennedy's accent, which to us seems an important part of the whole thing because neither Eisenhower nor Nixon has an accent like Kennedy's, and even though we are all from Massachusetts, most of us don't either.

"Okay, cats, so he said, 'Let the word go forth from this time and place, to friend and foe alike, that the torch has been passed to a new generation of Americans . . .' So who is he talking about, man?"

"Us!" we all scream. "He's talking about us."

"Really? Donnie."

"He is talking about how we are going to be in charge. A new generation taking over."

"Really, cats. But dig this. He says, 'Born in this century, tempered by war . . .' Is that you?"

"Yes!" we all scream.

But I can see that he isn't talking about us. He is talking about himself and about our parents—about the World War II people. Why is the torch being passed to them? Haven't they had the torch already? Now it is our turn. Why not take the torch while you are young enough to enjoy it?

"But have you been tempered by war?" Mr. Walter questions.

"Yes," says Rocco Pizzutti. "So far our whole lives have been about war."

"Okay. I can dig that. So what is this? Kennedy says, 'We shall pay any price, bear any burden, meet any hardship, support any friend, oppose any foe, in order to assure the survival and the success of liberty.' What is he talking about? Are you ready to pay any price? What price are you going to pay?"

"Whatever price we have to pay," says Stanley. "So we can all be free."

Everyone cheers. And we are ready, ready to bear the burden and pay the price. We will assure the success of liberty. We are ready to stand up to our foes. We are ready for John and Jackie. Men used to wear hats but John Kennedy doesn't wear one and so we will not wear hats. He is the future.

We are all talking about these things in school, about the torch being passed and not wearing hats and paying any price and how Jackie is beautiful and speaks French. I don't know why everyone likes her speaking French so much. We have started French in school and we don't want to have to speak it. Maybe being beautiful and speaking French is a good combination.

But I heard other things in Kennedy's speech that I didn't talk about just then. No one would want to. Everyone was too excited. But Mr. Walter talked about them anyway, pointing out that Kennedy said, "The world is very different now. For man holds in his mortal hands the power to abolish all forms of human poverty and all forms of human life." Mr. Walter looked around the room and said, "What's that about, cats?"

"Do we really have the power to abolish all forms of human poverty?" I ask.

"Of course we do," says Donnie, sounding annoyed. "And Kennedy's going to do it." And the class cheers again.

"But aren't we spending more time and money on the other stuff?" I ask.

"What other stuff?" says Kathy Pedrosky in a voice that makes it clear she thinks I am disgusting.

I don't want to be disgusting to Kathy Pedrosky but I

want to understand. So I keep going. "Why are we building things to abolish all forms of human life?"

"What are you talking about, Joel?" asks Kathy, pronouncing my name like it is the dumbest sound she ever heard. I want to just drop the whole thing. But she insists, "What?"

"The bomb. The A-bomb."

The class laughs, possibly because my voice breaks when I say "A." It comes out in a high squeak.

I don't want to talk about it anymore but it is bothering me. Kennedy mentioned "the deadly atom" and "mankind's final war." Is that what my war is going to be? A final war with nuclear weapons that ends the world?

It is funny that just as Kennedy arrives and fills us with hope, I am starting to think about a lot of things besides the Yankees and the Republicans, and a lot of those things are really scaring me.

I ask Dickey Panicelli what he thinks about World War II and the bomb because he is older and knows about things. His long hair falls over his face and he throws it back with his hand before he speaks, giving him a James Dean aura, James Dean being the actor whose aura we most want. You want to know what someone thinks who can do that with his hair. Only it is hard to hear him over his lawn mower engine. He says something about "the Communists" and I guess that makes sense. We have to stand up for what is right. The Germans didn't, and they allowed concentration camps. We can't be like that. We have to be willing to pay any price to ensure the survival of liberty.

I am not the only one thinking this stuff. We all talk about it—World War III and the end of the planet. There is a movement called "Ban the Bomb." Shouldn't the atom bomb be banned? Mr. Shaker, who is my teacher this year, says that we want to ban the bomb but can't because the Russians have it. Russia is the big problem because they are Communists. Nobody will explain to me what Communists are. Most people say they are people who want to take away freedom. But some say they want to share everything. The first group must be right, otherwise why would we pay any price to stop them? But I wish I knew more because everyone says that the next war is going to be with the Communists. Actually, a lot of people say we are at war with them now, but it is a "cold war." "Cold" means no shooting. But that is just for now.

Does paying *any* price include destroying the entire world? Most of my friends don't want to talk about that just now. Kennedy is president and everyone is feeling good and excited. When I ask these kinds of questions, the other kids seem to get angry. So I avoid the subject—which, I suppose, is what everyone else is doing too.

Instead of asking questions, we form a club. We call ourselves the Three Musketeers, after a book we are supposed
to be reading though it is a little too long. Stanley and Donnie and I are the Musketeers and Jackie Kennedy is Queen
Anne. We vow that we will fight together and pay any price
together and that, when the time comes, we will all go into
the same branch of service at the same time, though we can't
agree on which branch that will be. We give ourselves secret
names, the names from the book. Donnie is Athos, Stanley
is Porthos, and I am Aramis. We start calling ourselves by
these names but only when no one else is around. There is
a fourth character, D'Artagnan, and I suggest that we let
Rocco be D'Artagnan. Athos and Porthos agree but Rocco
says the whole thing is stupid, which is upsetting for me
because Rocco was the only other Brooklyn Dodgers fan.
But we all know that the character who is really missing is
the beautiful Constance. In the book, they all loved Constance. We do not have a Constance.

CHAPTER SIX
LOVE IN THE COLD WAR

I have the Cold War to thank for Kathy Pedrosky. Kathy Pedrosky has eyes that are the same green as the deep ocean. Looking into them makes you confused. Her lips are thick and soft-looking and always seem like they are about to kiss someone. Why not me? All the girls in the neighborhood wear dresses, but Kathy Pedrosky wears skirts—little tight skirts.

My relationships with girls have mostly failed. Rocco Pizzutti said I could go out with his sister, Angela. Rocco approved of me because I stood by Sal Maglie and the

Dodgers. But Angela was a pretty version of her brother and that wasn't going to work. When I looked at her, I saw Rocco.

About then I noticed something appealing about Susan Weller. Actually, what was appealing was that she had beaten up Tony Scaratini. He came to school with a blackened right eye and the story got out that Susan had done it.

But it soon became clear that Susan Weller was a horse—or at least she thought she was. If you spoke to her she would let out a high-pitched neigh and gallop away. I almost suffered the same fate as Tony. It turned out that if you cornered Susan Weller, in my case to ask her why she was making horse noises, she reared up and snorted and pounded you with her fists as though they were hooves.

My mother didn't think any of these girls deserved me. The only one who was good enough for me, according to my mother, was Myrna Levine. Myrna, my mom pointed out, was extremely beautiful. She did have nice black eyes, though really, when it came to black eyes, Angela Pizzutti's were better. But my mother pointed out that Myrna was "extremely intelligent," which was Mom's way of saying she was Jewish. She may have been extremely intelligent—she got good grades—but it was hard to tell because she just giggled about everything. She clung to Kathy Pedrosky, and whenever anyone said anything she would lean over to Kathy and whisper something and then giggle. It may have been my mother always pointing out Myrna that led me to noticing Kathy Pedrosky.

Kathy Pedrosky doesn't giggle and she doesn't neigh, she speaks. She speaks a lot. She ran for student council; she is in debates. And in addition to her cute little skirts, the lips, all that—this is a girl I could really talk with.

But she doesn't talk to me.

If only I could talk to her. But I can't. What can I say to someone that beautiful? Can I ask her to console me about my continuing grief that the Dodgers have moved to Los Angeles, which at first I thought was a different part of Brooklyn? California was something I could not understand. How could they move to California? Weren't they from Brooklyn? It is not as though Brooklyn and California are the same thing. Do they even play baseball in California? Don't they all have blond hair and smiles? No one on the Dodgers looks like he is from California. I am certain that Sal Maglie and Roy Campanella don't surf.

No. Kathy wouldn't understand. I could have talked to Angela about that, but not Kathy, and it is Kathy I want to talk to. Could I talk to her about my fear of nuclear war, something I am thinking about all the time now? No, she would not like someone who is afraid, even though it seems to me that an exception should be allowed for being scared of the total destruction of the planet.

Maybe I can talk to her about the Kennedys. We all like talking about Jack and Jackie. This is Massachusetts.

But when I start to talk to Kathy she looks at me with her jade eyes. The LePines went on a car trip to the Rocky Mountains and Donnie came back with these dark green stones—one for him, one for Stanley, and one for me—for Athos, Porthos, and Aramis. It was jade, Montana jade, and the rocks were to be the symbol of our special bond.

Kathy's eyes were the color of Montana jade and when she looked at me, I couldn't speak. One time Tony Scaratini took my pen. I was going to tell him to give it back but before I could say a word he punched me in the stomach and I felt so sick I couldn't speak. I couldn't even breathe for a few seconds. Kathy Pedrosky's green eyes have the same effect on me.

✕ ✕ ✕

This morning the siren is sounding. It often does and we know exactly what to do. We all get under our desks. Or anyone's desk. It is a quick scramble like when the music stops in Musical Chairs. But you don't want to be the one who's out because it might be a nuclear war. So we all dive pretty hard for a spot.

We are preparing for the day when the Russians hate us

so much that they decide to come over and drop a nuclear bomb on our school. I am not sure why, of all the schools in America, they would pick ours, but it is better to be ready. Mr. Shaker says, "In the next war, the front line could be right here!" Why would Haley be the front line? It wasn't the front line in anything. Even in the French and Indian War Martin Haley had to go up to Canada.

We know what nuclear weapons could do. We have seen films of that sickeningly slow mushroom spreading upward—something evil eating up the sky. We see films over and over again about the Nazi concentration camps and the nuclear bombing of Hiroshima and Nagasaki at the end of World War II. It is a little strange, these two subjects, because the one had been done by Nazis and the other by us. But we have to do it—because of Pearl Harbor, my birthday.

Because we have seen these films of the bombed cities in Japan, we do not think hiding under desks with our hands over our heads is really going to work. It is hard to see how this is a safe hiding place from the destruction of the entire planet. We don't talk about this, but somebody must be lying to us, and it is probably the school.

There is a lot of talk about being ready to hide in the basements of our houses with enough food and supplies to wait it out until the radiation is gone. The Panicellis built an elaborate shelter with a door that can be shut so tight,

Dickey says radiation cannot get in. Popeye and Dickey built it. And Mrs. Panicelli filled the shelves with gallon jugs of water and cans of food, especially tomato sauce and boxes of dried spaghetti. They are prepared to live on spaghetti and survive the destruction of the planet.

It bothers me a little that my family is not prepared. We have not built anything in the basement though there is a closet there, where my parents store canned food and wine. We had always called it the "cold storage" but when I ask my parents about a shelter, they claim that this is it and we all start calling the cold storage "the shelter." My mother says, "Joel, could you go down to the shelter and bring up two cans of tuna fish?" There is no water in the shelter. Only wine, vegetable oil, cans of lima beans, and an inexplicably large supply of canned tuna fish. This worries me.

I suppose, when the attack comes, the Panicellis will let us in. The Wiszcinskis also have a well-supplied shelter. The Wiszcinskis always have a lot of food, which is surprising because Stanley is so skinny. Stanley did not think much of the food in our shelter and told me that when the attack comes I could come to his. I could even bring Sam if I wanted. We clicked our pieces of Montana jade and smiled.

So when the attack comes I will have a number of possibilities. Hiding under a desk, on the other hand, is hard to take seriously. We are told to do it and we do it. You have to do something to be ready for the Communists.

When the alarm sounds, Stanley Wiszcinski often dives under the same desk as I do. We look out from the bottom of the desk to see Miss Norris's legs. They are an architectural wonder. She is so fat that from her knees to her ankles her legs are all the same thickness, like two pillars. And then all of this is held up by shoes with the thinnest, highest heels imaginable. They must hurt her.

"How can she stand in those shoes?" Stanley whispers to me.

"They're going to snap," I say.

"When she comes falling down we'll be safe here under the desk. See, Joel, it's safe here." We both start laughing.

"You won't be laughing when the Russian Communists come with atom bombs," Miss Norris snaps. She's right. That is not going to be funny. But now I recognize Myrna Levine's giggle and know that Kathy must be nearby.

"Are your hands over your heads?" Miss Norris says in a threatening tone. We quickly put our arms back up, at that moment more afraid of Miss Norris than the bomb.

✕ ✕ ✕

But today when the siren goes off and I dive under a desk, instead of Stanley being there it is Kathy Pedrosky. And Myrna is nowhere in sight. I don't know what to say. Of course, we're not supposed to be talking, so I don't have to say anything. But it is an opportunity, if I could only think of the right thing to say. Something good could come from the Cold War.

But what? I know she will not be interested in Miss Norris's legs.

Then Kathy Pedrosky turns her eyes to me and says, "Joel, I feel safe here with you."

I want to say something. I almost say "I feel safe with you too." But then, just in time, I remember that this would be a huge mistake. I am the man. She doesn't want to make me feel safe. I am supposed to save *her* from a nuclear attack. I think of saying something like "Don't worry, I will save you." Save her from the Russians. But how do you save someone from a nuclear attack? So I do not say anything.

After school she is standing by the front door—just standing there, as if she is waiting for me. She holds out her hand and I take it and we walk out together holding hands.

Now I am mostly thinking about Kathy. I take my allowance and buy a pin with a gold circle, which she wears. I feel grateful to the Communists in Russia.

CHAPTER SEVEN
MY CUBAN LOVE CRISIS

I was grateful to the Cold War for getting me Kathy but then it took her away. I suppose I can blame Khrushchev.

Nikita Khrushchev, who looks like my uncle, bangs his shoe on the table and can't go to Disneyland. That is what I know about the head Russian, Nikita Khrushchev. It does not seem like enough to hate the man, unless it is true that he wants to drop an atomic bomb on our school. No one likes an A-bomb dropper. But I don't believe that he does, and in fact he never has dropped an A-bomb on anyone. We did, but he didn't. I just don't understand this Cold War. It is between the free world and the Communist world, and the Communist world wants to make us not free. But a lot of dictators are on our side, including the one in Spain who used to be a friend of Adolf Hitler.

There are only two facts about Khrushchev that I know are true. One day at the United Nations, in front of television cameras, he took off a shoe and banged it on his desk to drive home a point. They show this on television from time to time and it always makes us kids laugh. But adults want us to take it more seriously. One day in school Mr. Shaker says we all have to write essays about Russia, and Stanley takes off a shoe and pounds it on his desk. We all laugh but Stanley is sent to detention.

The other thing I know about Khrushchev is that he was not allowed to go to Disneyland. I am not sure if this was punishment for pounding his shoe. I find that hard to believe but I wouldn't have believed he really did pound his shoe if I hadn't seen it. I only know that he was visiting the United States and he wanted to see Disneyland and they turned him down.

But now something else has come up with the tough bald Russian leader. It turns out that he is ready to use nuclear weapons to destroy the world because of Cuba. For an instant I think I finally know why I am supposed to hate the Communists. The problem is that Kennedy is ready to do the same thing.

The Russians started it. They put nuclear missiles in Cuba. Now we have to make them take the missiles away. We could get their nukes in Cuba with our nukes, but then they have more nukes to get us and we have plenty more to get them. It sounds like the games we used to play as kids.

So now I go to bed at night wondering if I am going to wake up in the morning. Or will I be "the last man left," like in a movie I saw about the only survivor of a nuclear war, wandering the earth finding nothing but dead people. Or would it be like another movie I saw, in which lots of people survived but they were all dropping over, one by one, from radiation.

I know that I am angry probably because I am scared and because I don't want the world to end over Communists. Kennedy is ready to blow up the world, but he has already gotten to do a lot of things. He has gotten to marry Jackie and drive a PT boat and be elected president. But what do I have to show for my life now that the world is about to end, now that "life as we know it"—they always use that exact phrase—is about to end? I have held hands with Kathy Pedrosky and have been punched in the stomach by Tony Scaratini. I am thirteen years old so I have barely gotten to be a teenager. I want more time than that. Even if it means leaving missiles on the island of Cuba.

And what about that island? Isn't Cuba a little island? What would it be like to be on a small island with all the world's nuclear weapons pointed at you? The kids in Cuba must be even more scared than we are. They really do have nuclear weapons pointed at their school.

Nobody talks about the Cubans. It is only about the Americans and the Russians. Everything is about the Americans and the Russians. No one else matters. As for the Cubans—the Cubans are Communists, so everybody figures they have it coming just like the Japanese had it coming because of Pearl Harbor.

What is it all for? We fought the Germans and the Japanese because they were evil. But as soon as we beat them, they were our friends. So couldn't we just skip ahead to that point? Couldn't we say, right now, "The Communists are our friends," and skip the part about the nuclear war?

I say this to Stanley and Donnie. I even say that President Kennedy is going to get us all killed. But they are not listening. They take out their green stones and talk about "getting the Russians." I click my stone with theirs. I am promising to get the Russians too.

We talk about the situation a lot in school. I don't say much. I might if someone else was saying things that sounded anything like the things I'm thinking. But I am alone. No one else is having these thoughts and that tells me something.

Somehow I have taken a wrong turn that no one else has taken and I am going to be quiet about it until I understand how I have gotten it all wrong. In my school, you don't say bad things about President Kennedy. Not in my school. Not in Haley.

"So, cats," says Mr. Walter. "What are we going to do about Cuba?"

Donnie LePine is right there with his hand straight up in the air, snappy like a salute, proud that he knows the answer. "We have to make the Russians back down."

"Nuke 'em! Nuke 'em right in Cuba!" shouts Stanley Wiszcinski. All those early years spent surrendering the Japanese flag have somehow damaged Stanley's mind.

"We have to stop them," says Kathy Pedrosky. She always says everything so well. If only I agreed with her. But I just keep quiet. A lot of the kids agree with her. They don't like the idea of the Communists pushing us around. But I don't see them pushing us around. Khrushchev just wanted to go to Disneyland. Well, he also wanted to have a lot of missiles—as many missiles as we have, and we want to have a lot of missiles too. But why aren't the other kids talking about life as we know it ending on the planet?

I can see that, despite what they say, a lot of them are worried. The whole school is acting like Rocco Pizzutti, somber and silent.

The school gives us regular updates on the situation and I can tell that the teachers are scared too. That makes me feel better but also worse. I am glad that I am not the only one scared, but it also confirms that I have good reason to be scared. Wouldn't it be better if I were just crazy and weird and there is nothing to be scared of?

Kathy is scared. I can tell by the way she hangs on to me. I like that. But today, for no reason, she starts crying. I lie and tell her it will be all right.

She cheers up and says, "President Kennedy will know what to do." I nod, but I don't want to answer because I am not at all sure that is true.

✕ ✕ ✕

And then suddenly it's over. The Russians back down. I'm glad that someone has.

"There is no stopping America," Stanley says.

"Not as long as we have President Kennedy," says Kathy. "He knows how to handle the Russians."

"Are you sure?" I say. "He nearly got us all killed."

"But he didn't," says Kathy. "And now we're a lot safer."

"I don't feel safer. Life as we know it on the planet could end." A look comes over Kathy Pedrosky's lovely face. It is disdain. "Kathy, you were scared. We both were scared."

"Joel, you can be so creepy," she says. And she walks out of the room with Stanley Wiszcinski.

I had been right in the first place. Girls don't like guys who are afraid of things. Even if they are just afraid of the end of the world.

CHAPTER EIGHT
A LIVE GERMAN

I remember my father once saying "The more money you have, the more money you can get." This, of course, is very bad news for poor people. Well, there is also some bad news for lonely people: the more friends you have, the more friends you can get.

Ever since the Cuban missile crisis, when Kathy declared officially that I was creepy—and everyone heard her—I haven't been popular. Let me be clear. I am fourteen years old, well into my teenage years, and for teenage boys, popularity means being liked by girls. I still have my friends Athos and Porthos. We click our stones and talk about fighting the Russians and even debate whether we will do this from the army, the navy, or the air force.

I am not sure about fighting the Russians but these are my friends and I don't want to be alone. The winter of my unpopularity would have been the perfect time to meet someone new, but that was not when Karl Moltke showed up. Instead he came along in the spring after I made my comeback.

I owed my new standing to the correct application of my two pinkies. It had started during baseball practice. Mr. Bradley watched me at bat and then called me over. "I told you what your problem is," he said while his fingers kneaded the sinew in his damaged shoulder as though he were looking for something lost in there.

I knew the problem. He had been telling me all spring. I gripped the bat too tightly and it choked my swing. I tried to loosen up but every time the pitcher stared at me, my fingers tightened.

"That's why they stare at you like that, Joel," said Mr. Bradley, still searching through his shoulder.

"I can't help it."

"Tell you what you do. Hold your pinkies out."

"What?"

"Just try it."

He had me swing the bat with my little fingers pointed out and suddenly my swing felt so easy that when I connected with a ball it just leaped off the bat into the air to the far end of the park and beyond.

I have become a home run hitter. I have more home runs and a better batting average than Donnie LePine. Of course he is still a better fielder and a better base runner. But everyone loves a home run hitter. I am going to get a varsity letter, a big orange letter that you sew on the pocket of an ivory-colored buttoned sweater. There are twenty-five team members and twelve varsity letters. I have never gotten one. Tony Scaratini always gets the one for my position. But maybe not this year.

We have a good team this year because Mr. Bradley finally realized that Rocco Pizzutti is not a third baseman. Mr. Bradley stood on the mound, fingers working his shoulder, and said, "Come over here, Rocco." He turned him toward home plate and told Stanley to hold up a mitt. Then Rocco pulled back his left arm and threw.

Stanley screamed and dropped the glove in pain. And that was it. Rocco has become a pitcher. No one can hit him. No one even wants to be standing there when he throws—not the batter, not the catcher, not even the umpire. If the catcher misses and the pitch hits the backstop fence it gets stuck there, wedged in the chain links.

This is my first winning team and my hitting streak is one of the reasons why. Mr. Bradley smiles at me and jokes with me. All my teammates want to be around me. Girls want to be around me, though Kathy still thinks I'm creepy. Suddenly Susan Weller is talking to me and not just neighing and spitting. And I notice that she doesn't look a bit like a horse. She looks very nice.

I enjoy my new standing. Of course I will have to learn soccer and get a lot better at basketball if I want to maintain this position all year—like Donnie, who has varsity letters in all three sports.

I might write about this in my diary. For my birthday my parents gave me a red leather book with a strap across the pages that locks with a small brass key. Every few weeks I carefully unlock the book, examine its blue-lined empty pages, and just as carefully lock it up. I do this over and over again. I have for months now. But I've been thinking that I might write about events. What Fidel Castro said that day. How the astronaut training program will someday send the first men to space—if the Russians don't get there first and make the moon Communist. How Ted Williams hit three home runs in the same day for the Red Sox. I have become an enthusiast for power hitters now that I am one. And who else is there to root for, now that the Dodgers are gone?

Or I could use this diary as an imaginary friend to talk

to about the things I can't talk to my friends about. Like my fear of nuclear war or the shape of Susan Weller's no-longer-horselike body. Maybe I should write about sex. I've been thinking about it a lot and I am not going to talk to anyone about it.

I don't know how to write a diary.

The most famous diary, the one I have heard the most about, was written by a girl not much older than me, named Anne Frank. Anne Frank was a German Jew in hiding with her family in Nazi-occupied Amsterdam. She wrote in her diary while in hiding. She wrote about her family and the other people in hiding and her thoughts and her feelings. She could express herself. Her diary was her friend. And all of it is particularly stirring because I know that in the end, no one will save her. Someone will give up the hiding place, the Germans will come and take the family away to be gassed to death, and no one will do anything to help them.

I start spending late afternoons after baseball on the screened-in porch, lying in a glider, a sort of rocking couch, reading the carefully written feelings of this German girl, soon to be killed by Germans.

Suddenly there is the flat slapping sound of someone trying to knock on the screen door. With my book still in my hand, I walk over to the door.

There stands a boy of about my age, with short-clipped

dirty-blond hair and gray eyes. I have not met many foreigners but I can tell that he is one. His haircut, half-inch spikes of hair sticking out evenly all over his head, is not an American haircut. His baggy gray shorts pulled in tight at the waist and ballooning out around his thin legs are definitely not American. Nor are his leather sandals with long straps that wrap several times around his bony ankles.

"Hello," he says with a slight accent. "My name is Karl Moltke. I am zeh new Gehman exchange student."

He explains that he is staying with the Hargroves. They live down the street but I don't know much about them because they don't have any kids. I think Mr. Hargrove was in the Pacific.

Karl holds out his right hand to shake mine and I quickly take the book into my left hand and hide it behind my back, hiding Anne Frank from the German. As we lock hands to shake, he gives one stiff jerk and nods his head, at the same time swiveling his feet to make his heels hit each other. After a childhood of German ghosts, this is my first live German.

CHAPTER NINE
TAKING A STAND

Mom," I say. "This is Karl. He is from Germany and he is living here now."

My mother extends her hand but Karl does not take it. Instead he makes a slight bow and swivels his feet so that the sides of his heels slap together. My mother backs slightly away from him. I look across the lawn at the Panicellis' house. Popeye Panicelli might shoot him if he acts like that. What is Mr. Shaker going to do when he sees Karl click his heels? The new exchange student doesn't know it, but he's in danger. He needs to be a lot less German to live in Haley. I better teach him quickly.

I teach Karl how to shake hands, not to click his heels, and how to dress. I will have to teach him baseball. That is the quickest way to be an American. But as I think about it, baseball is not that easy to explain. In the fall there will be soccer and he will probably be the best player in school. Germans are good soccer players. That is the answer. Soccer will be his savior, just as baseball had been mine. In my school, it doesn't matter how smart you are. None of the other kids care what kind of grades you get. Good looks are not that important. Where your family came from, how much money they have, what your father did in the war, the clothes you wear—all that is secondary. But if you play a sport well, you are in.

✕ ✕ ✕

This summer I am teaching Karl how to act more American, starting with a good batting stance. The other kids don't treat him badly. They always call him "Kraut," but they use a friendly tone. "Why don't you put the Kraut in?" Rocco and the other pitchers shout from the mound. They all do the same thing. They blow two pitches right past him and then with a two-strike count, instead of striking him out, they fire a fastball right into his left shoulder. It doesn't hurt him very much except when Rocco is pitching. Karl never has enough sense to get out of the way. He seems to think it would be unmanly to dodge a pitch. Besides, he likes being hit because it means he can go to first base and he knows that he would never be able to hit a single. He isn't a very good base runner and he almost never scores. His running has improved a little since I got him to get rid of those weird sandals and get some cleats.

✕ ✕ ✕

I thought things would start going well for Karl once soccer season began. But something terrible happens. We are walking to school together, and just before we enter the school yard I see Tony Scaratini just standing there, smiling. Tony doesn't smile very much and when he does it is never good. As we approach he raises two fingers to his smirking upper lip as though they are Hitler's mustache, thrusts his other hand straight into the air, and shouts, "*Sieg Heil!*"

It is the Nazi salute. He is calling Karl a Nazi. What difference does it make? Tony Scaratini is the biggest jerk in the school. Everybody knows that.

Except maybe not the two kids by the gate to the school yard who seem to think that Tony has made a great joke and are now doing the same thing. More and more kids join in. We are surrounded by dozens of boys mocking Karl, making fun of him for being German. Karl just looks at the ground and keeps walking.

The same thing happens on the way home from school and on the way to school the next morning. It happens twice every day. Mr. Shaker seems to see it. You can never tell with him but he is standing in the doorway of the school watching kids make fun of Karl, calling him a Nazi and shouting "*Sieg Heil!*" Looking at Mr. Shaker, I think he is very angry. As I get closer I can see that he is shaking a little bit.

"It isn't fair, is it, Mr. Schacter?" I say, thinking for once there is something we can agree on.

Mr. Shaker's eyes look like he can see for hundreds of miles. All he says is, "Who can say what is fair after what they did?"

I want to say that Karl hasn't done anything, but I am late and have to get to my homeroom. At my locker there is a group of boys giving Nazi salutes and telling Nazi jokes. Stanley is there and he laughs uncomfortably at the jokes.

"It isn't fair," I say. "Karl didn't do anything." But the other kids just laugh. And then Stanley, still smiling and looking uncomfortable, says, "Ah, Aramis, have you gone over to the Cardinal's side?" And he looks around for approval but the other kids ignore him because they do not understand. I do, of course. The Cardinal was the Musketeers' enemy.

Karl isn't going out for soccer. He wants to spend as

little time at school as possible. I tell him that it might make a difference if he did well at a sport but he only says, "It's not even an American sport." He is right. Playing soccer better than everyone else would be like wearing weird clothes or having an accent.

✕ ✕ ✕

Dickey Panicelli has moved up from go-karts. He is working on a big eight-cylinder engine in an old green-and-white Chevy, black grease smudged on his white T-shirt, his long sandy hair falling in front of his eyes as he leans over.

"Dickey, did you ever notice the way they treat Karl?"

"The German exchange student—" He says more, but he revs his engine and I can't hear it.

"But it's not fair, don't you think?"

The engine shouts, covering Dickey's voice for a few seconds. ". . . the whole problem with Germans. They can't stand up for things. My father says that if a few Germans had stood up and said Hitler was wrong there would not have been a World War II."

"But I thought it started because of Pearl Harbor."

I can't hear his answer. So is that it? Not standing up against something wrong is so bad that even the children who had not yet been born are guilty? Maybe that is why

I have to stand up for Karl. He didn't do anything. Probably his parents didn't do anything either. I want to stand up for him but I also don't want to because this is the kind of thing that can turn the whole school against you. Karl's is not the side to be on.

I wonder what my uncle, whose whole life seems to have been shaped by killing Germans, thinks. I tell him the entire story and he says, "Do you know what the Germans drank?"

He insists on waiting for an answer. "No," I say.

"Ice wine, Joel. Wine made from ice. We moved into this *Schloss* and the cellar was full of this *Eiswein*. We drank three bottles a day. It was pretty good stuff."

My mother says that there is no such thing as a good German, that they are all bad. But I don't see how that is possible. "Karl didn't do anything," I insist.

"No," my mother says, "but what about his parents?"

My father has gotten into the habit, when he wants to talk to me, of saying "Let's go to the shelter and get some tuna." Down we go, and we lightly stroke the roundness of the cans while we talk.

"Even if the Germans didn't do anything," my father says, "there are times when not doing anything is a crime too." He seems to think this is an important point, something he wants me to get. But I am wondering why we have so much tuna fish.

I need somebody to help me, to help Karl. I write about it in my diary but, of course, a diary never answers. Mr. Bradley is younger than the World War II generation and increasingly I feel that if you want to talk through something you need to talk to people who haven't been in World War II.

Mr. Bradley says that I am right, that it isn't fair. "You should have him come out for baseball this spring. Tell him that there are not going to be any *Sieg Heil*s on my ball field."

I wonder if I could talk Karl into it. Baseball is a long way off. It is still soccer season. I say to Karl—we have never really talked about it—"I think it is so unfair the way these kids treat you. You didn't do anything. It wasn't your parents."

He looks at me with his gray eyes pale as chalk.

"Your parents didn't do anything, right?"

"As a matter of fact . . ."

"What?"

"My *Vater.*"

"What about your vater?"

"I don't know. I never knew him. After zeh war, zey were going to put him on trial. Za Americans. For sings he did."

"What did he do?"

"I don't know," Karl says. "But he killed himself. I was a baby."

I am quiet for a very long moment trying to think of what I can say.

"You know," Karl says, "it's very funny. I must tell my *Mutter* when I write her."

"What's funny?"

"Isn't it funny zat I come to America and everyone treats me badly because I am German and zeh only one who is nice to me is za Jew. Za only Jew I've ever known."

We both smile uneasily.

✕ ✕ ✕

Karl never makes it to baseball season. He writes his mother and tells her the "funny" thing and suddenly Karl is packed off. His only explanation is that his mother told him he had to go back to Germany. I don't know if she is calling him back because the other kids treat him badly or because his only friend is "the Jew." What is his mother like?

I have another big-hitting baseball season and I am getting a varsity letter and Tony Scaratini isn't getting one. His response is to try to club me with a baseball bat. He takes a good swing but I move out of the way and he misses. You can never please everyone. But maybe I should stand up to him more. I do not want to be like a silent German. Since Karl left I have been thinking a lot about Germans. Shouldn't

I have said something more to him? It's bothering me. In a way I am glad he left so that I won't have to stand up for him, but that is bothering me too. Finally I have something to write about in my diary. I write a lot about the Germans, which is funny because my diary inspiration, Anne Frank, did not write much about them at all.

CHAPTER TEN
MY DIARY

November 23, 1963

Dear Diary,
    I know that I have not written to you very much. I started but then I stopped. I can't do this every day, but today I wanted to write to you because yesterday was a different kind of day. I went to school and it seemed like a normal day and then, on my way to lunch, I passed Mr. Bradley, the baseball coach. We have become pretty good friends, especially since my batting average has gone up, but I was

surprised when he motioned to me in a kind of secretive way to come talk to him. It is November and baseball season is a long way away. What could Mr. Bradley have to talk to me about?

He opened the door to an empty classroom. Everyone was heading for lunch. He turned the lights on and looked at me as though he hadn't decided what he was going to say. And then he said it.

"I've just heard over the news that somebody has shot President Kennedy and Governor Connally of Texas."

I looked at him. He was not joking. Is this how it all ends? How could this be? "Is he dead?" I asked.

Mr. Bradley shook his head. "I don't know." He looked down at the floor for a moment without saying anything. Then he said, "I've got to go." He walked out into the hallway.

He would be all right, I thought. John Kennedy is not going to end this way. Not now. I must have stayed in the room for longer than I thought because when I came out Mr. Bradley was nowhere in sight. I walked through the hallway looking at faces and it was easy to tell who knew and who didn't. Even Tony Scaratini had a worried look on his face. He had never had that face before—he generally looked too stupid to be worried—and that new face told me he knew. But Donna Belini, who had been interested in me ever since I started hitting home runs, didn't know. She had a big smile for me that I didn't want at the moment.

Mr. Shaker looked angry. It was the way he always looked so I could tell that he didn't know. "Mr. Schacter," I said. "President Kennedy has been shot."

He looked at me as though I had shot him and he started shaking. He said, "Is that supposed to be funny?"

"No," I said. That was all I felt like saying. He looked around as though he was looking for help. I guess he was looking for another teacher, a grown-up, someone he could trust. All he saw was Mrs. Harmon, the math teacher. Mrs. Harmon turned everything into a math problem. If you asked her what time it was she would say something like "Ten minutes ago it was 11:57." If you asked her when the homework was due she would say "There are eight problems. I expect each one to take a day and a half."

Everyone avoided talking to Mrs. Harmon. But she was the only grown-up Mr. Shaker could see and so he turned to her. But she did not give him a puzzle, she just nodded her head. It was true.

Then I realized that Mrs. Harmon was crying. And Mr. Shaker was too.

For some reason, I was looking for Susan Weller. Since you are my diary, I will be honest. I wanted to be the one to tell her. Everybody will remember who told them and I *wanted Susan Weller to remember it was me, which is not what you should be thinking about at a time like this. I will only tell this to you. But then I saw Angela Pizzutti. Her face was wet and shiny, not just a few tears running down. She was covered in tears and her eyes looked up at mine completely red where they should have been white. She just grabbed me and held on to me and I held on to her. I liked her for feeling so much though a lot of people were holding each other that day. It felt good to be holding someone because I felt really scared. But that is another thing that I am only telling you, Diary. I am not going to make that mistake again.*

I was the one who told Donnie LePine. We will both always remember that. He was looking smooth, in charge, the way he always looks. And then I told him and for the first time ever he looked lost, confused, scared like me. We held on to each other for just a second or two, long enough for me to realize that there was still a truth to our old Musketeers joke—for all his varsity letters, we were friends, guys of the same age with the same struggles and the same frightening future. Even if we can't really talk about it.

President Kennedy didn't get better. He died. And a lot of people are crying. When I got home I could tell that my mother had been crying. My father didn't say anything when he got home and I couldn't tell if he had been crying too.

And so, dear Diary, I am writing to you today because I realize that yesterday was the last day of my childhood. The last day I will ever believe that things might go right. They might start to, but someone could just take a gun and end it. Maybe that's what people do in this country. They have weapons, they have missiles, they have armies, and wars, and they kill people and that is how they end everything. That doesn't really make any sense. I can't think clearly. That is why I am writing to you, because if I told anyone else the things I'm thinking they would just get mad. My fellow Musketeers would say I was betraying them.

Some people thought that John Kennedy was hope. I wasn't so sure. To me, President Kennedy was not a sure thing. He just offered the possibility that the future would be better. And even if you didn't feel that hopeful, he was the only hope we had. So now we have nothing. Who will they shoot next? I think bad things are going to happen. Thank you for listening to me. I will try to write you more often.

Joel

CHAPTER ELEVEN
THAT ONE WRONG SWING

They say every baseball player has taken one swing that he wishes he could take back and try again. The one that is always talked about is Willie McCovey's swing that made the last out of the last game of the 1962 World Series. Matty Alou was on third and Willie Mays was on second. The Giants were beating the Yankees one run to zero. Any kind of outfield hit could have scored both of them and won the series for the Giants. It was one ball and one strike so McCovey didn't have to swing. He could wait for the right pitch. But he swung and drove it straight to the second baseman and lost the series. For me it was all made right the next year when the Dodgers, thanks to the unbelievable arm of Sandy Koufax, swept the Yankees in four games. It ended the Yankees and I don't even think about them anymore. But I'll bet Willie McCovey is still thinking about that swing.

The swing Tony Scaratini wants to take back is the one at the end of last season when he missed my head. He is never going to forget the varsity letter that I got and he didn't. All fall he stares at me in silence. He seems to be angrily confirming that my head is intact. He is dreaming of taking one more swing and this time connecting.

Leaving homeroom, he walks up to me and says, "I'm going to see you after school." That is all he says after seven months of thinking about it but everybody knows what he means. My only question is whether he is talking about fists or if he will be waiting for me with a baseball bat.

I don't look forward to fighting Tony. First of all, because he is certain to fight dirty. Also, because he is bigger than me and meaner than me. What makes it even worse is that the weather has just turned cold. It is too cold to be standing outside hitting each other.

I am on my way into science class and I see Tony. "Listen, Tony," I say, "it's really cold outside. Why don't we put this off until spring? Baseball season."

Scaratini's lip curls when he sneers. It is the sort of thing you can't fake. Only genuinely mean people can curl their lips like that. All he says is, "Be there. Don't make me come looking for you."

There is no backing out. By this point, everyone knows that we are fighting after school. I've never understood how it works, but news of a fight travels very quickly. Already several people have come up to me to offer support. Donnie says, "Show him what you've got, Joel." Nobody really likes Tony. Maybe that's what makes him so mean. Besides, most of the kids are certain that, as the saying goes, I can take him. I may be the only one who doubts it. And Tony, I guess. Everyone else reasons that I am now the better baseball player, a varsity-letter winner, so I can take him. That is the whole problem: I got the letter instead of him. In fact, I realize now that I may have provoked this whole thing by wearing my letter. My parents had bought me the cream-colored cardigan, the stadium sweater that all letter holders wear, for my birthday, and my mother sewed the letter on and I had worn it to school for the first time the day before. Was that what provoked him?

Whatever the consequences of fighting him, they would be better than the consequences of not fighting him. With the whole school knowing about the fight, there is no way out. Even if a few people don't know, as soon as the two fighters face each other on the field, kids will run through the school yard shouting, "Fight! Fight!" Most of the boys stand around in a circle, cheering. Kids like to see a good fight.

The girls, of course, don't come, and I don't know what they think about fighting. It is one of the mysteries about girls. They often express contempt for boys fighting. But if you don't fight, if you back away from a fight, there is probably not one girl in the whole school who will ever talk to you again.

No, whatever happens, it will be better than not fighting.

Rocco Pizzutti comes up to me in science lab and whispers, "Let me take the jerk for you, Joel."

Rocco owes me because I decerebrated his frog for him. This is a really weird thing. It is supposed to teach you how the brain works. You place a scissors blade inside the mouth of a live frog and cut, snipping off part of the frog's head. Then you watch the thing hop around with its head chopped to note how differently it acts with a piece of its brain, the cerebrum, missing. Who wouldn't act differently?

Weird! Who thought up that one? Tony Scaratini?

Anyway, Rocco Pizzutti, for all his toughness, can't do it. He holds the frog firmly so that it can't jump around, placing the scissors blade sideways in the frog's mouth. He starts to squeeze the scissors and he feels the little body in his hand tense up. He can't do it. It's because he doesn't do it quickly enough.

And you have to do it. Mrs. George, who has long, bright red fingernails that look like she has been using them for decerebrations, makes it clear that "everyone *must* decerebrate" at least one frog. So I do Rocco's and quickly hand it to him and he stands there holding the animal with the chopped head, looking sick.

"Put it down, Rocky," says Mrs. George, who knows her science but can never get Rocco's name right. "See if it will jump."

"It's too late for that," says Rocco sadly.

He is grateful that I have done it. But I can't let him fight Tony for me, much as I would love to see Scaratini trying to sidestep Rocco's murderous left.

"No thanks, Rocco," I whisper. "If I did that, every bully in the school would challenge me just to see me back down so he could feel big."

"I'd take them on too. I'll be your protector. Anyone wants to take you on, he has to answer to me. There won't be many."

"Thanks, Rocco. It won't work."

"Well, you can get him."

"Thanks, Rocco."

"Yeah. How are you and Angela getting along?"

Since the Kennedy assassination, every time I see Angela, she starts talking about Kennedy, about how it was a plot. It seems obvious to most of us that something odd was going on. They arrested this strange man named Lee Harvey Oswald. We all wonder who he was and why he wanted to kill President Kennedy. But before we could find anything out, this guy named Jack Ruby, who knew a lot of criminals and was dying of cancer anyway, walked up to Oswald and shot him right on TV.

I don't know what the adults are thinking but every kid can see that the criminals hired Ruby to kill Oswald before he could talk about how he didn't shoot Kennedy. Maybe he would have even said who did. But Jack Ruby made sure he couldn't talk. We can all see this, but Angela has gone far beyond that and she can't stop talking about it. If I see her and say, "Hi, Angela," she will grab my hand and say something like "Campisi—ever hear of the Campisis? One of them visited Ruby in jail." She whispers this to me as though it is a secret I am not to repeat.

I am finding it very hard to be around Angela. But this is not a good time to point this out to her brother. Fortunately, before I can answer Rocco's question about getting along with Angela, Mrs. George raises one of her flame-red dagger nails in the air and says, "No talking." No one argues with those nails.

As the day goes by it becomes increasingly certain that there is no way around this showdown with Tony Scaratini. When the final school bell rings, I walk to my locker, resigned to my fate. Donna Belini comes up to me so serious and sincere that I can barely stand it. She gives me a hug, as if saying good-bye.

While I am at my locker putting on my coat and looking for my gloves to protect my hands, Susan Weller comes up behind me and pats me on the back. I jump and knock into the corner of the locker door, which bruises my cheek. Marked before it even starts.

CHAPTER TWELVE
OFF-SEASON HERO

With my coat on and my gloves pulled tightly over my hands I walk outside, the same way I do every day. Only this time a crowd of kids follows me out as if they are accompanying a boxer into the arena. First comes Stanley Wiszcinski, looking very serious. All of them look serious, in fact. Fighting is a serious business at my school and you don't joke around about it. Rocco Pizzutti comes up from behind and smacks me on the back and whispers, "Listen, Scaratini is a moron. All he is going to think of is hitting. He has no intellect for counterpunching. He will take his shot and then, when he's off balance and exposed, you can just pop him."

The air is so cold that it burns my face. My cheeks sting and my eyes are tearing. I probably look like I am crying. The more I try to wipe my face with my coat sleeve, the worse I must look.

Stanley seems very excited about the fight, like it is a sports event he has been looking forward to. He wants to click green stones and seems disappointed that I am not carrying mine into battle. We are fifteen years old and Stanley is the only one of the Musketeers to still carry his piece of jade. He leads me through a big crowd of kids. In the center is Tony Scaratini, with the curl in his lip, wearing a big green corduroy coat lined with thick fluffy off-white wool. It is a good coat, a warm coat, but not a coat to fight in. You can't move in it. But Rocco is probably right that Tony is too dumb to think of moving. I, on the other hand, am wearing my fatigues, the olive-drab army field jacket that my uncle was issued for the Battle of the Bulge, a jacket designed for moving fast in one of the coldest winters in history. It is still a little baggy on me but it fits better than it used to.

Stanley starts running around the yard shouting, "Fight! Fight!" The crowd is getting even bigger. Tony Scaratini is a person who did not hesitate to club someone with a baseball bat so it is probably good to have lots of witness when you fight him.

He is glaring at me, which is how you are supposed to begin. Then he smiles, more a kind of smirk. "You look scared," he says.

"I'm just cold," I protest.

"Come on," he says. And the crowd starts shouting.

"Show him what you can do, Joel," Rocco hollers.

Tony throws the first blow, a big round stupid pendulum swing just like Rocco predicted. I try to step out of the way but my legs are stiff from the cold and I trip and fall on one knee and tear my pants, my new chino pants that my mother just bought me.

Now I am angry. Why do I have to be standing out here in the cold, tearing my brand-new pants, because some moron wants to trade punches? He wanted it, I didn't. Why do I have to be here?

I stand up and wait and, sure enough, he throws the exact same punch again. This time I neatly sidestep the blow and let fly with a hard right straight to Scaratini's mouth. Serves the imbecile right.

The next thing I know, I am in the worst pain I have ever experienced—that woozy kind of pain that makes you feel sick. It's my hand, my frozen hand. I had hit him really hard. Tony is on the cold ground spitting blood from his mouth. Have I really hurt him? He seems to spit out a piece of a tooth. I broke his tooth? "Tony, are you all right?"

But now the crowd moves and pulls me along. I am the

victor and everyone loves a winner. I may be more popular at that moment than after any of my home run games. All the girls smile at me and all the boys want to be my friend.

Well, not all of them. There are a few boys, the biggest, toughest ones, who make it clear that they want to "take me." When you have something good, people want it, and every bully in school wants the friends and admiration I have because I won a fight. They imagine how much they will be admired after they have beaten the hero.

X X X

The next day Brian Sorenstag, who never talks to me, is waiting outside French class and says, "I want to talk to you." Brian is the star of the basketball team. He is tall and blond and has the confidence of a champion. This is not as true during baseball season, but now it is winter and in the wintertime he is the untouchable champion in a sport I could never master. I had a hoop on the garage and I practiced over and over again until I could make thirty-seven out of fifty free throws. Real swishes right through the net. The problem is that this one shot is all I can do—no hook shot, jump shot, or dribbling. I made the team but was rarely put in a game. So Sorenstag sees me as a loser who sits on the bench. Only now, in *his* season, everyone is talking about me as some kind of champion because of the way I hit poor Tony Scaratini, who no longer speaks to me, not that he ever had anything to say. Scaratini the bully simply vanishes. It shows how sometimes fighting really works. Just like the way the Germans and the Japanese were stopped.

But now I have to fight Brian Sorenstag—also Jimmy Kelly, Tom Davis, and Ronnie Decker. They have all asked for their turns in the school yard. I tell Sorenstag that my hand is too sore from hitting Tony. He is always worried about his hands during basketball season, so maybe if I remind him that he could hurt his hand he will be less eager to fight. But he just says, "I'll give you a week." I tell the others that they will have to wait until after I finish with Sorenstag.

What am I going to do? There is no end to this and I hate it. What is the point? Either you lose with a sore mouth or win with a sore hand. I'm not even sure which is better. Isn't Tony Scaratini better off than me? Maybe I should make sure I lose the next fight so that I won't have to fight again. But you don't just lose the fight, you lose everyone's respect. And where I go to school, losing respect can be a dangerous thing.

I ask my father what he thinks I should do.

"Joel, let's get some tuna," is his answer.

Down in the shelter he says, "It's not good to fight." He

thumbs the cans as though just discovering their shape. "No one wants to fight. But sometimes you just have to."

"Dad, didn't you hear me? No one wants to fight? There are a lot of kids who want to fight. And they are all lining up for their turns!"

"Just make sure you don't start it," Dad says.

I guess he wants to help, but he doesn't seem able to understand the situation I'm in.

I ask the baseball coach, "Mr. Bradley, can I talk to you about something private?"

"Sure, what's on your mind?" he says.

"I got in a fight with Tony Scaratini."

"I heard!" Mr. Bradley says with great excitement.

"You did?"

"I heard you laid him out in the first round. Tough kid too. It was about time."

"Yeah, but now the problem is that a lot of other kids want to fight me."

"Well, you took care of Scaratini. You'll do fine."

The last thing I want to do is disappoint the baseball coach, so I just leave. He pats me on the back as I walk out the door.

In desperation, I decide to try Mr. Walter.

I explain my predicament to him and he says, "Oh, man, what a drag. Are you going to fight all these cats?"

"I don't want to."

"Okay, dig on this, man. This can be a major moment in your life. Like, all your life, cats have been telling you that you have to do what you are told. Do you know what that gets you, man? That gets you Germany."

I think about Karl.

"Oh, man. You can do whatever you want. You don't want to fight, don't fight."

"But how do I do that?"

"It's your show, baby."

I like the way he talks even though I'm not always sure what he is trying to say. One thing seems certain. If I keep fighting, there will be one after another after another.

✕ ✕ ✕

I tell Brian Sorenstag that I am ready to fight him. "Found the courage, huh?" he says contemptuously. That makes me want to show him. For an instant I dream of the glory I would bask in after I destroyed Brian Sorenstag. And I think I might be able to do it. He is bigger than me but he is gangly with long arms and if I went inside he would be lost.

I enjoy the dream briefly and then I remember what happened when I beat Tony Scaratini. They were all waiting to try to "take me." After this it will be even worse. I know what I have to do.

"Fight! Fight!" Stanley Wiszcinski starts shouting around

the school yard like a town crier. He doesn't need to. This is a showdown between the guy who took Tony Scaratini and the star of the basketball team. Everyone wants to see it.

Out on the field with the crowd surrounding us, steam coming out of his nose into the cold air like the pink, steaming nose of a cow in a winter field, Brian looks a little taller, a little meaner, his arms a little longer. But his arms will tie him up. I'm sure of it.

He throws a long right hook, a perfect shot for me to get inside him on. But instead I stand there, flat-footed, and throw off the blow with a flick of my right arm. It doesn't feel like much of a punch. He throws the same one again and I do the same thing. He tries a right and I push it away with my left.

"Come on," he demands.

"I'm not going to hit you," I say.

"What are you afraid of, Bloom?"

"It's stupid and I don't want to do it. I don't have a problem with you."

"Oh, you are chicken." He throws another right. To show my contempt I don't even try to block it. It lands on the side of my head and doesn't hurt. There is nothing in his punches. I put down both my arms and let him swing—right, left, right, right. He is breathing heavily—clouds are billowing out of his mouth. I have him. It is working. And then, disaster.

Rocco Pizzutti impatiently shoves his way into the middle of the circle and unleashes his left, sending Brian sprawling on the frozen ground.

"Jeez, Rocco, why'd you do that?" Brian is almost crying.

"You want to hit someone, hit me!"

"I don't want to hit you, Rocco."

So why, I wonder, does he want to hit me? I am standing there in the center of the circle but no longer a part of the scene, feeling sorry for Brian Sorenstag. Also feeling sorry for me.

Later I say to Rocco, "Why'd you have to interfere?"

"I wasn't going to stand there and let him hit you."

"Why not? I was winning. Didn't you see that?"

"Winning," he says, rolling his eyes. "The guy was using you for a punching bag."

"And he was all punched out."

Rocco's face suddenly breaks into a smile. "Then you were going to nail him down?"

"No. Then I was going to walk away."

"That's why I hit him."

"Who asked you to interfere?"

Thanks to Rocco, I now have a fight a day. They all want to see if it is true that I won't fight. It *is* true. Once it becomes clear that Rocco Pizzutti is not going to interfere again, I start drawing kids who are looking for a safe chance to win a fight. They are no good at all. I stand there with my arms down and they swing away, timidly at first, and then more freely once they feel reassured that nothing is going to happen to them. But they don't know how to hit and nothing hurts me and there is no glory in hitting someone who just stands there and doesn't fight back. Soon everyone gives up on fighting me.

That is what I wanted but now I am beginning to wonder if it is worth the price. No one wants to talk to me. Stanley avoids me. Donnie smiles pleasantly at me but seems far away. Even Rocco doesn't have much to say. Angela Pizzutti is polite but doesn't tell me about the Kennedy conspiracy anymore. Donna Belini doesn't want to be seen near me. Susan Weller never looks in my direction. When Myrna Levine sees me she doesn't even giggle. Should I tell my mother there's no chance for Myrna anymore? I suppose they all have their reasons. No one wants to discuss it, so I don't know exactly what their thinking is. But I kind of do.

✕ ✕ ✕

My little brother, Sam, comes home from school and, without saying a word, closes his fist and throws a hard punch that lands on my chest. I am getting used to being hit.

Actually, he throws a better punch than most of the big kids. It turns out my brother is mad at me because now he has to fight all the time because kids are curious to see if he will fight too. I tell him that if he shows them he won't fight, kids will stop challenging him. But his only response is to throw another punch in my direction.

I know that once baseball season starts again, if my batting is good, the whole thing about not fighting will be forgotten. Until then I'm going to school and coming home and spending my time next door at the Panicellis'. I am living like a German exchange student.

I am helping Dickey work on a 1957 Chrysler, two-tone, turquoise and white. We have a hard time with the push-button transmission but finally get it working, and we rebuild the huge eight-cylinder Hemi engine. It takes two of us to handle, disassemble, and clean the giant 360-cubic-inch engine block and replace the gaskets.

Mrs. Panicelli brings us little sugary Italian cookies. Popeye comes home in the late afternoon and talks about the Communists. He hates Communists. "The damn Communists."

"Honey." Mrs. Panicelli reprimands him for his language. Soon he vanishes inside the house.

I feel safe in the company of the Panicellis and it makes me feel good to have engine grease on my hands. At the end of the afternoon we wash up with this special glop for taking the grease off. But I don't work at it very hard because, in truth, I like having a little black grease showing. My parents don't like it, though, and always send me back to the bathroom at dinnertime to wash my hands again.

I have made a deal with Dickey. In exchange for helping him with his Chrysler, he spends time pitching me balls so that I can practice hitting. I hope the Red Sox are doing the same thing. Even on the coldest days, I swing as long as Dickey is willing to throw pitches. Next spring has to be my best season ever, and with some practice it could be. Thank God for baseball.

CHAPTER THIRTEEN
EXPLOSIVE ELEMENTS

May 18, 1964

Dear Diary,

Once again I want to write down something I really can't tell anyone because it is so weird. Here it is. I love Mr. Shaker's chemistry class. There are two things that are wrong about this. One: nobody likes Mr. Shaker, and two: nobody likes chemistry. The chemistry teacher was Mr. Balard, a quiet man. He was so quiet that I could not hear anything he said. He would stand in front of this large chart of the elements and talk very quickly in a soft voice. Then something miraculous happened. Mr. Balard left. He just left and nobody told us why because they thought kids were too stupid to notice that Mrs. Pudheiski, the home economics teacher—who was so beautiful that all the guys kept saying they were going to take her course though none of them ever did—also left. And Mr. Pudheiski, the assistant principal, stayed, seemed sad, and started giving a lot of detentions. Why did they think we couldn't figure this out?

But that's not why I am writing this. Mr. Shaker is filling in as chemistry teacher, and even though he is easier to hear, this is very bad news. Chemistry is bad enough without getting it from Mr. Shaker. I had him for history and I hated it the exact way that I always knew I would hate having him as a teacher. And now here he is in the chemistry lab and he's even moved in his stupid Yankees banner.

However, I have started to understand that the chart of elements behind him is actually very interesting. To begin with, many of them are extremely unstable and given to exploding. Sodium, for example, is a soft metal that tends to explode and give off hydrogen gas when mixed with water. It is interesting that so many of these elements are given to violent reactions because the elements are what everything in the world is made up of, and so many are violent. Take hydrogen. It is very dangerous, given to burning and to exploding. But Mr. Shaker says that hydrogen is the most common element, that 90 percent of the atoms in the world are hydrogen. No wonder the world is a dangerous place.

But these explosive elements can be tamed by mixing them in the right compounds. When hydrogen is mixed with oxygen, you get water, which is very stable and puts out fires. Sodium can be mixed with chlorine, which is poisonous, and it makes salt. So when you look at a chart of the world broken down to its basic elements, the world looks dangerous. But it turns out it is just a matter of how you mix things up. Now I realize, after wondering for a long time, what I will be. I am going to be a chemist.

Mr. Shaker, in his white laboratory coat, faces the class and demonstrates the explosiveness or stability of compounds. He mixes things in glass test tubes that he holds over the sink. Sometimes they turn bright colors; sometimes they give off smoke in different colors. Often they make a little pop and then the test tube shatters and a colored stain appears on Mr. Shaker's white coat. He flinches when the test tube breaks and then looks sadly down at the sink and says, "Isn't that a shame." You never know if he is saying that about the experiment, the broken test tube, or the stain on his coat. Or is it about the way he flinches? Or does he just think it's a shame that the kids are all laughing?

I have a chemistry set and I try to do some of these

experiments at home. I tell my little brother, Sam, that we are going to have a chemistry class and learn to explode things. He gets very excited and sits in front of me full of expectations. I model myself after Mr. Wizard, a television character that was popular when I was little. On the show, Mr. Wizard spoke very quickly and demonstrated dazzling science experiments. Only all of mine fail. I cannot produce even one explosion. Can I ever really be a chemist? Sam tells our mother that I promised explosions and haven't produced anything. My mother has taken away my chemistry set.

You know, I try to work with Sam, but he doesn't make it easy.

CHAPTER FOURTEEN
THE FIRST NIGHT OF MY WAR

It is early August, the height of baseball season. Koufax is still pitching no-hitters for the Dodgers, but the Cardinals, the Reds, the Phillies, and the Giants all look good. The Yankees are also looking good, but so are the White Sox. The Red Sox are nowhere in sight. Maybe I should have stuck with the Dodgers, but to me the Dodgers aren't the Dodgers anymore—just some team in LA using the same name.

The Red Sox are beginning a three-day series with the White Sox tonight. It's on the radio but not on television and Boston will probably lose anyway. A movie about the

Battle of the Bulge is being shown on television and my uncle has come over to watch it with my brother and me. We have all snuggled into our places, my uncle in the overstuffed chair where he will seem to be asleep until suddenly he will utter something in a low voice.

We have all settled in, but it is too early for the movie. We turn on the television anyway and watch the *CBS Evening News with Walter Cronkite*. The show is a favorite of my parents'. Walter Cronkite has the world's best voice and seems to know everything. He narrates a lot of shows about World War II that I have watched with my uncle. I have learned more about World War II from Walter Cronkite than from my family.

Tonight there is news from a place called Tonkin—the Gulf of Tonkin. Lyndon Johnson, the president who replaced Kennedy but who is not young or charming, is on television. The president has a slow, soft, southern way of talking that makes everything seem a bit boring and unimportant.

"Last night I announced to the American people that the North Vietnamese regime had conducted further deliberate attacks against U.S. naval vessels . . ."

I'm only half listening. I can tell by the sound of Johnson's voice that this is nothing important or even interesting.

"Communists," my uncle mutters.

What have the Communists done now? Why are they

always making trouble? This time it is the Vietnamese, the North Vietnamese. It seems to me that I have heard of this place, Vietnam, before. It must be near Laos, which is somewhere in Asia and has been in the news a lot. It has always seemed like a poetic name—Laos, the Laotians. "Vietnam" and "the Vietnamese" do not sound as beautiful.

Some of our navy ships had been attacked in international waters. Johnson says that he ordered an "air action" against the boats and facilities that were used in the attack. The air action has already taken place, he says, "with substantial damage to the boats and facilities."

Wait a minute! What are they saying? "Substantial damage." Johnson can slowly drawl anything away, but I know what he means. Suddenly I am seeing the whole thing. We have done substantial damage and they have shot down two American airplanes.

This is a war! Just like World War II: soldiers attacked, damage was substantial, and airplanes were shot down. There were people in those airplanes and they are probably dead. And it is not going to stop there. Johnson has asked Congress for a resolution "supporting freedom and . . . protecting peace in Southeast Asia."

I know what "support freedom" is going to mean, though I am not exactly sure what is meant by "Southeast Asia." Where is Southeast Asia? Somewhere near Laos, I guess.

I can hear the seriousness, if not in President Johnson's steady melting voice, certainly in the curt way Walter Cronkite is talking about it.

Nothing seems changed. The evening news ends on schedule with no special programming or announcements like there were in the Cuban missile crisis or when Kennedy was shot. But I think this is very important news.

The movie comes on. German tanks roll across the snow and American infantrymen trudge along in retreat. Whenever a place name comes up my uncle quietly repeats it. "Malmédy," he says as if trying to memorize it, though of course he will never forget it. His life, his mind, were changed by this place called Malmédy.

But I'm thinking about a place called Vietnam. Suddenly I realize something about this place. I realize that this is going to be my war. This is the war I have always known was coming. It will not be called World War III as I had often thought and as was often said. It will be called Vietnam. And it will change my life. I am fifteen. I still have two and a half years before registering for the draft, but Vietnam will be there waiting. I am going to be asked to support freedom and protect peace in Southeast Asia—at any price.

It isn't going to be exactly like this movie. I don't know what it will be like, but I know that there will be no snow and no Germans. Maybe it will be more like my father's war in the Pacific. But it is going to be a war. I am watching the actors shooting and killing and ducking for cover. I keep asking myself, "Could I do that?"

I look at my uncle, watching the movie with his eyes shut. Someday I will sit in an overstuffed chair in front of a television with my eyes shut and repeat softly the word "Vietnam."

CHAPTER FIFTEEN
HERE IT IS

Here it is, my war, and I don't understand anything about it. I never thought it would be like this. My father and all those other fathers had a war they could understand—a fight over who was running the world. But now I can see that my war isn't going to be a world war to make the world safe. It can't be because of nuclear weapons. Now wars have to be small and mean and fought over little strips of land you might never have heard of a year before. Just because we can't have any more world wars doesn't mean we can't have war. So it turns out that their war didn't make the world safe after all.

Everyone at school knows that somehow this is about us. The news has never before been about us; it was always about our parents. We thought Kennedy was passing the torch to us, but then we found out he was passing it to them—and to himself. But suddenly, here is something about us. Adults aren't treating us any differently. They still act like our opinion doesn't matter. But we now know that what we think and do *will* matter. The adults just don't see it yet.

We have things to understand and decisions to make, and we have all started asking where Vietnam is and where Tonkin is. Angela Pizzutti is especially concerned.

"The Gulf of Tonkin is a big lie," she says, coming up from behind me in the hallway as I am putting my bulky social studies book from the last class in my locker. "It's a big lie, Joel."

"You mean there is no Gulf of Tonkin?" I ask with amazement. Rocco is standing behind his sister drawing circles at his head with a finger to indicate that he thinks she is crazy.

"You mean the place?" she asks.

"I looked it up," says Rocco. "I saw it on a map. It's in Vietnam, near Laos. All the same thing, I think."

"Well," I say, "that would explain why the Vietnamese are there. But why are we there?"

"Exactly," says Angela. "Why did they kill President Kennedy?"

"And why did they attack us?" says Rocco. "Were they crazy? Now we are going to really give it to them. What did they think would happen?"

"Maybe it's like Pearl Harbor," I offer, but I am not at all sure that is right.

"Suppose they never did attack," Angela says.

"Angela," says Rocco, throwing out his hands in exasperation, "it was on the evening news."

"So what," says Stanley Wiszcinski. "Remember them reporting the Orioles had lost when Brooks Robinson scored in the ninth?"

"That was just a mistake because the game ran late," I argue. "They corrected it later."

"Well, this isn't a mistake," Angela says.

"No, it isn't, Angela," says Donnie LePine, with the confidence of a man who has all the facts. Angela is stunned. She fixes her eyes on him. Is Donnie LePine actually agreeing with her? Everybody believes Donnie. Or is he just making fun of her?

"It wasn't a mistake?" I ask Donnie.

"No, but they did correct it later."

"What are you talking about?" says Rocco, who is also beginning to suspect that Donnie might be making fun of his sister.

"They've been arguing about it in Congress," says Donnie. "Turns out Johnson lied and there was no attack."

"Why would he do that?" I ask.

"So we can go to war," says Donnie.

I am completely confused. "Why does he want to go to war?"

"What?" Donnie asks, now looking a bit uncertain.

"Why does President Johnson want to go to war?"

Donnie just looks at me as though he is thinking of something else. He doesn't know.

"For the same reason they killed President Kennedy!" Angela insists.

"So what happens now?" Stanley asks.

Donnie is back in control. "So now they have to call the war off."

"Really?" I ask.

"Looks that way," says Donnie. Then the bell rings and everybody runs down the hallway to their next classes.

But Rocco and I stay a moment. "Good thing they're calling it off," he says. "We only have a couple of years before we have to sign up for the draft."

Rocco is right; it is a good thing. The whole mood of the school has changed. Everyone seems a little happy. Whatever happens, Vietnam is not going to be my war after all.

CHAPTER SIXTEEN
THE FIRST TO GO

But it isn't over. It is hard to say what exactly happened. Some say there were two attacks, some say one. Some say none at all. But why would somebody make something like that up? And why don't we know the truth? How can you be on a ship and not know if you've been attacked or not? There are a lot of arguments about this, especially in Congress, but they are going ahead with the war anyway.

I ask my father why this war is so much more confusing than other wars.

"Because you might have to fight it," he answers,

somewhat glumly, it seems to me. "War is very clear when someone else is going to fight it. It just becomes confusing when it's you."

"But the War was clear to you, wasn't it?" When you say "the War" it always means World War II. "I mean, you had to stop the Nazis."

He looks at me disapprovingly and says, "I was in the Pacific."

It is true—in the Pacific they were fighting the Japanese, not the Nazis. "Sure, I know, but the Japanese attacked Pearl Harbor."

He smiles a bitter smile. "Fighting the Germans would have made sense to me, but I didn't have to fight them. It probably made less sense to your uncle. Because he had to fight them."

"But wasn't Pearl Harbor clear? You had Pearl Harbor."

"Oh, it was clear. I remember before Pearl Harbor there were all these Jewish groups saying we had to fight the Germans. But no one agreed with that. Then after Pearl Harbor everybody agreed that we had to fight the Germans because the Japanese had attacked us. And that was supposed to make sense."

I have never heard anybody talk like this before. "I'll tell you something, Joel," he says, examining the label on a can of lima beans. "In 1945 I was in the Philippines. I was a major by then and I was being driven by an enlisted man in a jeep going through a mountain pass. Somewhere in the mountains was a Japanese sniper. You know, an expert shot with a rifle hiding far away and picking people off. Maybe he wasn't a very good sniper, because he kept missing. But you could hear the bullets hit the rocks. *Ping. Ping.* And it occurred to me that he was shooting at me because I was a major, and maybe I should take off my maple leaves. Or somehow cover them up. Or hide them. 'But maybe that would be an act of cowardice,' I thought. *Ping. Ping.* And maybe if I appeared to be the same as the guy who was driving he would shoot at him instead of at me. But then if he hit him, it would be my fault. *Ping. Ping.* Then again, he was already in danger because of me."

"What did you do?"

He doesn't answer. He is suddenly fascinated by lima beans.

My father has just told me a war story. It is the only one he has ever told me. There will probably never be another. But I have to say something to stop him from staring at the beans like that.

"How come we only have tuna and lima beans?"

He examines my face quizzically for a second while he struggles back. "Your cousin Bennie."

"What about Bennie?"

"He's a wholesale distributor for lima beans and tuna fish. Big deal."

And he goes back upstairs.

✕ ✕ ✕

Maybe it is a question of personality. Some people can see wars clearly and other people are confused by them. Or maybe it is just that some people are clear and others are confused in general. Maybe I am just a confused person. Other people don't seem to be having this problem.

I talk to Donnie LePine about Vietnam because he is the least confused kid I know. He is getting annoyed with me for not being like him. "Listen," he says, "it's pretty clear."

"It is, Donnie?" I say, genuinely struck by this. It is what I have been afraid of—it's clear to everyone but me.

"Yes. You don't need all these questions. Your country goes to war, you have to be there to help. That's all."

This doesn't clear things up for me. "What about the war being a lie?"

"The attack may have been a lie," Donnie explains. "But the war is real. And we can't let the Communists win."

Clarity isn't working. Who are the Communists anyway? Maybe I need a more complex view.

I ask Mr. Walter what he thinks. "Those are the questions,

man," he says, bowing his head to punctuate that thought with falling hair, which gives him the opportunity to throw it back on the next statement. "You cats better start asking those questions. I'm not going to give you the answer. You have to come up with your own answers. Dig on that, man."

Things are clearer over at the Panicellis'. Dickey is signing up. "Because my country needs me. That's it," he says. "We aren't going to get pushed around by the Communists."

"Damn straight," says Popeye.

"Dear!" Mrs. Panicelli cautions him about his language.

"Well, straight. However the hell you say it. If we hadn't been so slow to slap back at the Germans, there wouldn't have been a Pearl Harbor."

Now, I don't understand that at all. Wasn't it the Japanese who attacked Pearl Harbor? As Dickey and I get the big Hemi engine back together with its parts clean and new gaskets placed on the edges and everything clamped in, he explains about the importance of standing up and fighting. I start to feel a lot better. Still, it is hard to believe that Dickey Panicelli is actually going to war. He is the first of us. We will all go, just like our fathers.

Seeing his son enlist in the military is affecting Popeye's walk. The difference is subtle, but I am sure I'm not imagining it. His elbows and knees stiffen and his back straightens and he walks as though marching on a parade ground, turning at an abrupt right angle to leave the garage and go into the house.

$$\times \times \times$$

Dickey has joined the marines and is training at boot camp. It is baseball season again so I wouldn't have been working on cars with him anyway. But still, I keep thinking how the first of us is already off training for war.

Then he is back, but only for a visit. In his uniform. A marines uniform with that great red stripe. I cannot help imagining how I would look in a uniform like this. I don't want to be a marine, but they do have that uniform. I have always thought of myself going into the navy because I like their uniforms, but I have to admit a marine could look pretty good. We have all discussed the different branches of service. Rocco wants army, which I think is a mistake because my father and uncle didn't seem to like it. Donnie and Stanley and I have been talking about the service since our Three Musketeers days. But we can never agree on where we are going to war together. Donnie likes the air force. Stanley likes the marines. A lot of these choices have to do with the uniforms.

I have to look closely to see that it really is Dickey because they have shaved his hair off, making his ears and eyes seem very large and giving a kind of intense, almost angry look to his face.

They really are sending him to Vietnam. I'm still not sure where that is. I ask him and he just says, "Somewhere in Asia, I guess." I look on a map and it isn't close to anything I know; it is a part of the map I have never looked at. When my brother and I were little we had a globe and we would spin it and stick a finger on it, and where the finger stopped was where we were going to go. Our fingers never landed anywhere near Vietnam.

The next day Dickey leaves. He doesn't seem worried, though his parents do. Popeye looks fierce and Mrs. Panicelli looks sad. But Dickey seems unfazed. I've seen kids look more nervous about going off to college. "It's the training," he explains. "I'm ready. You know, Joel"—he leans in closer because he wants to tell me something especially important— "you know, now when I hear 'The Star-Spangled Banner,' it means something."

I look at him and whisper back, "What does it mean, Dickey?"

He just glares at me. It is a stupid question, I guess. Why am I always asking stupid questions? But I really wanted to know.

PART TWO
MY TIME

CHAPTER SEVENTEEN
THE F-WORD

This year I will turn seventeen and it is a great year because the Yankees aren't even in the World Series. It is between the Dodgers and the Twins and the Dodgers started off in trouble because Sandy Koufax took the first game off for Yom Kippur. I didn't see that game anyway because my parents would not let me watch a game on Yom Kippur, one of the few Jewish holidays that we always observe. The other kids watched because they aren't Jewish but they all said it was a terrible game.

The first thing everyone was talking about was whether

Koufax should pitch in the first game. Stanley came to me to ask if Yom Kippur was that big a deal given the importance of getting the best pitcher into game one. I wished he would pitch but he wouldn't, and they lost that first game. But now that the holiday is over, Koufax is pitching complete games almost every other day and the series is tied for the final game seven, and the winner takes the series. Should Don Drysdale pitch or Koufax? Koufax is better. Drysdale was awful in the first game. But Koufax just pitched nine innings two days ago. Donnie LePine is insisting that it's too hard on Koufax and that starting Drysdale is "the only responsible way to play it."

"Don't give me that," says Rocco, who, after all, is a pitcher. "If he couldn't do it, he would say so."

I am about to point out that you could start Koufax, with Drysdale warmed up and ready to go if needed. But something out of the corner of my eye stops me. It is Dickey Panicelli. He is back. His hair is long and hangs down straight like something limp and damp. He has a mustache. He is wearing green marine fatigues. It strikes me how different his green clothes are from the army field jacket from the Battle of the Bulge that I am still wearing. It fits me now. But Dickey wears marine green and I realize that my generation is going to be wearing a completely different type of old used fatigues. But his eyes have that same dead look that my uncle's have when he watches television, that I see in Mr. Shaker, and sometimes in my father. Dickey was one of us—but now he is more one of them.

✗ ✗ ✗

Dickey uses the F-word a lot now. He uses it in places you can't, like in front of my parents and especially in front of his mother.

"Fuck this," he says.

"Dickey!" she shouts in horror.

"Sorry, Mom. What the fuck."

"Knock it off," says Popeye. "I thought the marines would teach respect."

"Is that what you thought the fuckin' marines teach? That's not it, Dad. They fuckin' teach you, though."

I can hear this from my window. There is something wrong with Dickey. But it takes time. My uncle and Mr. Shaker and the vegetable guy, all of them took my entire childhood to get just a little better, my whole childhood, and they are still struggling.

Night seems to be worse. I go to sleep and about midnight I wake up. I hear this sound, a strange long note. Then I realize it is screaming. It is Dickey next door, screaming. Why is he screaming? What has happened to him? I hear his parents go into his room. But soon a fight breaks out about his language or respect or something.

Poor Dickey. The next night I hear him screaming and I decide to go over there and talk to him. I quietly slip out the back door of my house. I don't know why I am trying to be quiet. He is shouting so loud it almost echoes in the night. No one is going to hear my footsteps. As I get closer I realize that he is screaming the F-word. Poor Mrs. Panicelli. For a while he screams it, then he starts crying it, sobbing it, then mumbling something, then suddenly screaming into the night again.

Between our backyard and theirs is a small chain-link fence, which I hop over. But now the screaming has stopped. Their house is quiet and I don't know what to do. I can't just knock on their door in the middle of the night. I walk up to the window of what I know is Dickey's bedroom and stand on my toes. I can see into the room. There is a light on and the room seems an awful mess, with sheets and clothes tossed across the floor.

Suddenly I feel pain in my right shoulder and hear a shout. The next thing I know I am lying faceup in the mud, staring at the shiny heavy rubber treads of Dickey's combat boot. He is standing over me with his boot on my face.

"Dickey," I say, as though trying to wake him up.

"Fuck, man. One short kick and I drive your nasal septum clear into your brain. You're fucking dead, man."

"Dickey, it's me."

"I know," he says with a smile, and helps me up. He is wearing a marine-green T-shirt that is completely soaked. He is sweating so much that he looks like he just stepped out of a shower. He tries to say something, but his teeth are chattering and he can't speak. He is shaking.

"You have malaria," I say.

"Ye-e-ah," he says, shaking so badly that the word comes out in about eight syllables. We walk over to the swing set in my yard where I used to play when I was little and we sit on the swings. I let him stay quiet for a long time. I know how to do this. Then finally I say, "Are you all right?"

"Fuck."

"Fuck yes or fuck no?"

He smiles and even laughs a bit. Then we stay silent for a little longer. I know he will start talking soon. He does. "It was the last mission. The last fucking mission. I was so short I wasn't even supposed to go. But I wanted to be with my buddies. How stupid is that?" He talks for an hour about his last mission. But I have no idea what he is talking about. I never find out the details of the mission. Only that he keeps reliving it in dreams. But I don't know what happened—I don't know about Dickey's war any more than I know about my father's war or my uncle's.

CHAPTER EIGHTEEN
MY WAR, DEFERRED

It seems like we have all run off in different directions. More kids from my class are going to college than ever before in the history of the school. The reason is that the only other alternative is to go to Vietnam and end up like Dickey. Lyndon Johnson is sending more and more troops to Vietnam and it seems almost certain that we will all be drafted and sent. If you are in college, they won't take you until you graduate. This is called a "college deferment." But a lot of the kids in Haley don't have the money for college and they will be going to Vietnam. There are state schools and there are scholarships. Donnie LePine easily gets scholarship offers from three different schools that everyone wanted to get into. Stanley is struggling to get money but thinks he will at least be able to go to a state school. I get into the school I wanted, Whiting College in New Hampshire, and my parents say they can pay the tuition. I am luckier than most kids. But the crisis is just being deferred for four years. Once we get our degrees we will be sent off. Of course there is the possibility that in four years the war will be over, but at the moment it looks like it is getting worse. Besides, that is not my destiny. This is my war and it is going to take more than a college deferment to get rid of it.

My parents send me off to college with more tears than the Panicellis shed when they sent Dickey off to war. My father takes me down to the shelter to touch tuna cans while telling me things like "study hard." He is more sentimental than I ever realized. My mother has done research and assures me that there are Jewish girls at Whiting. I am looking forward to seeing what kind of girls they have at Whiting but this is not something I want to talk to my mother about. Donnie LePine, while considering Whiting, told me that it was known for its beautiful women. I am excited about my new life and about leaving Haley, even if I am a little sad about leaving. I'm even sad about not having Sam to pick on anymore. In the tenth grade, he is slightly taller and larger than me and so serious that I am sure most people would think he was the older brother. He tells me, "Listen, Joel, be careful. What you do in college is going to shape the rest of your life." By the time he gets to college he probably will be older than me.

× × ×

As a freshman at Whiting College, I consider joining an officer-training program known as ROTC. There would be a few special courses and training and a uniform to wear once a week. At least this way when my time comes I could go as an officer. Only something Dickey Panicelli told me is making me rethink this idea of being an officer. He says that the regular soldiers are killing the officers. At first I think he is telling a story like my father's about the Japanese sniper shooting at him, but then I realize this is something different. American soldiers are shooting their own officers. They call it "fragging." Dickey said, "They fragged two fucking lieutenants in my outfit. First one came. He was stupid. They fragged him before he got everyone killed. The second fuckhead was just as bad. Gone. Gone." He repeated the word "gone" several times and then did the stare like my uncle.

This story was a revelation to me because I had always thought that an officer was a good thing to be. The officer training at my college is Air Force ROTC. That's not even a good uniform. I remember how we all jumped on Donnie LePine when he said he wanted to join the air force. One thing about Donnie, he always wanted to look good, and an air force uniform—blue gray and boring—was not going to do it.

But that was a million years ago, before I had heard of Vietnam. Now the only thing appealing about Air Force ROTC is that you can train to be a pilot. I thought being a pilot would be wonderful. It would be exciting to fly airplanes. But more and more, news was coming in about what airplanes did in Vietnam. They were dropping bombs everywhere and unleashing napalm, a chemical that causes fire to cling to people's bodies. That was not the kind of pilot I wanted to be.

In fact, I was having the same problem with being a chemist. What did chemists do now? They made things like napalm. Napalm was invented during World War II by a chemist at Harvard. It was the old story: take two things that in themselves are harmless—naphthalene and a carbon-saturated fatty acid—combine them in just the right amount, and you get this sticky stuff that burns like gasoline, sucks the oxygen out of the air, and kills everyone in a ball of fire. The wonders of chemistry! I went to a demonstration in upstate New York on a bridge to Canada—it's funny, but it's called the Peace Bridge—and we demonstrated against, DuPont, whose slogan is "Better Living Through Chemistry," for making napalm.

So being a chemist was like being a pilot. I couldn't do it. You had to be careful. Look at Albert Einstein. A pacifist who opposed war, he was one of the all-time greatest creative minds, completely rethinking how the universe works. He figured out that the speed of light never changes and can be used in a mathematical formula to derive the energy released from any mass. So what did the scientists do with this knowledge? They took a tiny amount of uranium and produced enough energy to level the city of Hiroshima and kill more than 100,000 people. That's what they used physics for—so being a physicist is even worse than a chemist or a pilot. The way the world is, you have to choose your career carefully.

✕ ✕ ✕

I seal my doom. It is December, and to celebrate the twenty-fifth anniversary of the bombing of Pearl Harbor—a major event for television and newspapers but also my eighteenth birthday—I register for the draft. I do it by mail, filling out a form in which I state, as clearly as possible, that I am a full-time college student. I receive a card in the mail with my student deferment. Life goes on, as it will for the next four years.

There are a lot of kids from Massachusetts at Whiting College but not from Haley. This isn't a Haley kind of place, and most of the kids here come from fancier towns in suburban Boston or New York. The truth is that before Vietnam and the draft, college had not been a Haley kind of place.

The only other kid from Haley who is going here is Donnie LePine. When he first made his choice he said he was excited about our going to school together. Once we got here, though, I did not see much of Donnie. I didn't know where he was. I checked to see if he had joined Air Force ROTC, but he hadn't. Then one night there is a knock on my door. Opening it, I see someone who at first appears to be Jesus Christ but who, on closer inspection, turns out to be Donnie.

College has changed Donnie as much as war changed Dickey—but maybe in the opposite direction. I'm not sure. Donnie's straight brown hair flows and swirls toward his shoulders and the thick black beard that covers the lower half of his face is neatly trimmed. He looks like an Italian Renaissance version of Jesus Christ. Donnie invites me to a meeting of a student group that is against the war in Vietnam. It is hard to believe that a kid from Haley would be in such a group. But on the other hand, I have been thinking about this for years now and I cannot come up with a reason to fight in Vietnam. The Vietnamese don't seem to be plotting to take over the world. Aren't they just plotting to take over Vietnam? And now I realize that I am not the only one, not even the only one from Haley, having these thoughts.

✗ ✗ ✗

At the meetings I see that these kids are a lot different from the kids in Haley. No one mentions baseball or the Red Sox, even though the Sox have finally integrated and started putting together a real team for next season. These kids have all read books I have never heard of, and they like to argue about them. There is a German writer named Herbert Marcuse. He has come out with a new book called *One-Dimensional Man.* I am the only person there who hasn't read it. I know I should but at the moment, to be honest, what has drawn my interest is not so much the ideas of Herbert Marcuse as the ideas of Rachel Apfelbaum.

Rachel is also a freshman. Her head is covered with endless, indecipherable dark curls. She is wearing a flowing flower-print dress that she says she made herself. She says she makes all her own clothes. She looks great in them. But not only is she beautiful and not only does she make her own clothes and keep up with the latest German philosophers, but she has—what I used to call when I was back in Haley—clarity. She knows the Vietnam War is wrong. She has no doubts. It is wrong and racist and has to be stopped. She does not have to take a breath or swallow. She is sure of it. She is explaining this to me at two thousand words a minute and I am nodding my head like it is a language I don't speak and I can't let her know I'm a foreigner. Then she says, "You know, Marcuse says that there have always been subversives throughout the whole history of thought."

"Well, yes . . . Does he really . . . I think this—"

She interrupts me. "Have you read *One-Dimensional Man* yet?"

Now, if some girl in Haley said that to me I would say "Come on." But it is the way Rachel says it. First of all, she gives me a smile that is like a gift, like a reward. What wouldn't you do to get one of those smiles? But also it is the way she says the word "yet." That word means that of course I would be reading Marcuse's new book. It is just a question of have I done it *yet*. There is no judgment. But because of this, I cannot bring myself to disappoint her. So I say, "I'm reading it now."

And she says, "How is it going?" Which surprises me because it acknowledges that reading Marcuse may not necessarily go well.

So I say, "Okay . . . I've got some issues with it."

Incredible. "Some issues with it." Where did I get that?

And then she says, "I do too. We should talk about this."

"Yes," I say, getting nervous about how well this is going. "Yes . . . we should."

"Tonight at seven o'clock?"

Rachel Apfelbaum has just asked me out on a date.

CHAPTER NINETEEN
CRAZY PEOPLE

Formal logic foreshadows the reduction of secondary to primary qualities in which the former become the measurable and controllable properties of physics." Yes, that is what Marcuse has written in his new book. In anticipation of my date with Rachel Apfelbaum, I run to the campus bookstore and buy it. Do I have "some issues" with this book? Only this: I have no idea what he is talking about.

Reading Marcuse reminds me of the novels I struggled through in high school French. Whenever I started to understand a passage it would then slip into the incomprensible.

I would underline the passages I understood because those would be the parts I could talk about. There are moments in Marcuse when I recognize some phrases and start to understand him and then he says something like "In advanced capitalism, technical rationality is embodied, in spite of its irrational use, in the productive apparatus." I can't argue with that because I cannot figure out what he is saying.

But it doesn't matter. It turns out that Rachel Apfelbaum doesn't really want to talk about Marcuse after all. She wants to talk about absolutely everything, and we don't stop talking for the rest of the year.

We go to antiwar demonstrations in Boston, in New York, and in Washington. The police seem to have trouble with our ideas. They slowly encircle us as we march, then they fire off canisters of tear gas, which burn your eyes and make you feel ridiculous because you are supposed to be standing up for your beliefs but you end up doubled over and crying. We try bringing sliced limes, which everyone says counteract the effects of tear gas. But they don't seem to help. We also wear helmets. Rachel and I have football helmets—she rolled her eyes contemptuously when I pointed out that they sold Red Sox batting helmets at the store in Fenway Park. But there are all kinds of helmets. Some demonstrators even have army helmets and it is starting to remind me of how we played war as kids. The reason we wear them is that after the tear gas the police move in with clubs and start beating us. Only there are so many of us that somehow the police never get to Rachel and me. But we can see demonstrators who don't have helmets getting serious head injuries.

Why do the police do this? A lot of people seem to feel really threatened by anyone who opposes war, as though there is some basic right that we are trying to take away from them. They live in a world where war is accepted and soldiers are heroes. But if Dickey Panicelli doesn't feel like a hero, no one wants to hear from him. And certainly no one wants to hear that I don't want to fight for my country. It goes against all their beliefs and they just want to beat us until we see things their way.

Rachel, with her clarity, sees it differently. She says the police beat us because they are pigs. I've noticed that she loves the word "pig." She never says "policeman" or "cop." It is always "the pigs." Is Popeye Panicelli a pig? Rachel, who calls for total revolution, has never known a policeman personally. We argue a great deal.

"Don't call them pigs."

"Why not?"

"They're just people," I say. "You call them pigs and it makes them mad."

"Tough."

"People don't act well when they get mad."

"Are you afraid?"

I can't believe it. Is this like Kathy Pedrosky all over again?

Rachel believes in violence. She says that eventually we will have to "take on the pigs." I know this kind of talk from Haley. How you have to fight. I suppose when we take on the pigs, our school friends will wish us good luck and tell us to "show them what you can do."

This isn't making much sense. If we are opposing war, opposing violence, why use violence to oppose it? Everybody seems to be going a little crazy.

This is true in Haley too. I go back to Haley for spring break and I bring Rachel to meet my parents. What will they think of her flowing homemade dresses, of her arguments from German philosophy, of her talk of total revolution? Is she going to call our next-door neighbor a pig?

But this is getting very weird. My mother and father are looking intently into her eyes, smiling, and nodding their heads. They love her. She is the first girl I have ever dated that they like. Now I realize why they didn't like Haley girls. The only thing they notice about Rachel is that she is Jewish, and this pleases them. She talks about "ten million people, armed and on the streets," and they nod and smile!

To me, Rachel sounds completely crazy. But everyone

else has gone crazy too. Popeye Panicelli has taken to walking around the neighborhood with his nightstick in hand, twirling it and swinging it and talking about how he is ready to "bust some heads." Dickey smiles maliciously and stares off at some distant hill that only he can see. My uncle has started target practice, or so he claims, with the old bolt-action German rifle, getting ready for "when the hippies come." I realize, though he doesn't, that he is talking about my girlfriend. He has heard her kind of talk somewhere and he takes it seriously. Will the next war be between my uncle and Rachel Apfelbaum?

✕ ✕ ✕

I run into Rocco Pizzutti walking by the mills along the river, lost in thought. He does not know what to do because the Detroit Tigers, looking for a young left-handed pitcher to develop, have offered to sign him. It is a different era. Baseball is not about the Dodgers and the Yankees anymore. Koufax is retiring. The Red Sox are hot with Carl Yastrzemski. The dominant teams are the Cardinals and the Detroit Tigers. And the Tigers want Rocco Pizzutti.

"Rocco, that's fantastic."

He doesn't look like he agrees. "Should I sign with them?"

"You mean drop out of school?"

"Exactly."

He doesn't need to explain. He is eighteen years old. If he drops out of school and goes into the minor leagues and does well, he can be a major-league pitcher at twenty-two or twenty-three, which is the age they like to get them. But if he leaves the University of Massachusetts, he loses his deferment and he will be drafted. For an instant it occurs to me—here's Rachel's influence—that if the war continues, baseball is not going to be able to recruit young players and then Major League Baseball, a powerful ally, will also oppose the war.

But meanwhile, what is Rocco going to do? If he leaves school he will be drafted and will go to Vietnam. If he stays in school it will delay his career three more years and then he still might get drafted into military service when he graduates. So it could be five more years before he can play and the Tigers wouldn't be interested in him by then. Finally he decides that if he has to go into the military, he is volunteering for Vietnam because that will make his army time a few months shorter, which, if he times it right, could mean a whole extra baseball season.

"If I sign up right now, I can be playing ball in a year and a half."

"I don't know, Rocco."

At least Rocco was one person who had not gone crazy.

CHAPTER TWENTY

TWO KARLS AND ONE CHE GUEVARA

The letter was forwarded by my parents. It was from Karl Moltke in West Berlin.

March 12, 1967

Dear Joel,

I hope you remember me. I am sending this to your parents because I don't know where you are. But here in Berlin I am thinking of you as we learn in the movement about the great struggle in the U.S. and I hope that we are now brothers in the revolution. In the words of Che, "If you tremble with indignation at every injustice then you are a comrade of mine."

I am coming to Boston for the movement. "I am not a liberator . . . The people liberate themselves." But I am coming to help. Are you going to the demonstration in April in Boston? We could meet there. Please write me and tell me how to find you.

Yours for freedom,
Karl

I show the letter to Rachel and explain the story. She points out that more than half of the letter is actual quotations from the South American revolutionary Che Guevara. I don't know what this means but certainly it is a good sign that Karl has not taken up his family's politics.

We are planning on going to the demonstration. Rachel has her little red Volkswagen Beetle, which we call the Maomobile because the Chinese leader is always waving red books and red flags. She is driving Donnie and me. Sam is meeting us in Boston to demonstrate with us. I have promised my parents that I will take good care of him and not let "anything happen to him." Of course, I cannot guarantee this at a demonstration, but I am able to get away with it because my parents do not acknowledge how brutal the police are—even if they don't mind Rachel saying it. Also they are comforted by the fact that Donnie will be there because Donnie was known in Haley as a kid who never got into trouble. It will be Sam's first demonstration and it will change him and help him to not be so straight. A good whiff of tear gas gives a kid perspective. I only have to persuade him later not to give our parents all the details.

What will Karl be like? How has he turned out? We arrange to meet at a small café off Commonwealth Avenue, where Boston University students spend hours in debate while lingering over twenty-five-cent cups of coffee. It was Karl's suggestion. I wonder how he knows about this place. It is dark and smoky but still I immediately spot Karl. He is three times as tall as he was when I last saw him and probably weighs the same. But on top of the long, angular, bony body is the same face with the same pale eyes. Only the blond scraggly beard is different. He is dressed in a blue beret and green army fatigues with the epaulets running off his narrow shoulders and down his arms. I suppose the beret is intended to make him resemble Che, which he doesn't because he is too tall and thin. The green fatigues resemble the Cuban uniforms of Fidel and Che but it is clearly someone else's West German uniform because the name "Spieldorf" is printed on a breast pocket. I can't help but think about him wearing a German army fatigues jacket that he hopes will look Cuban while I am wearing American fatigues worn to kill Germans.

He recognizes me too and throws his long arms around me. "I knew we would be brothers in the revolution," he says. I am not sure why but I always find this kind of talk embarrassing. I introduce Rachel, and Sam—who doesn't remember him. Donnie does but Karl is not sure he remembers Donnie. We all sit down for a coffee and Karl expands on his revolutionary theory, which seems to involve killing a lot of people—"a million atomic lives." I look at Rachel and she confirms with her eyes that he is quoting Che again. But she and Donnie seem to be largely agreeing with Karl while I can't help thinking, "Why only a million and not six million lives?" But I am not going to say that and Sam says nothing. He is mostly looking around the café with great curiosity. I can see that he is impressed, that for once he thinks his big brother does interesting things.

We all go off to the demonstration together, comrades in the revolution, agreeing that if it gets violent and we get separated, we will meet back in the café—except that I cannot let Sam out of my sight.

Of course, it does get violent. Not too bad. A lot of tear gas and some clubbing. A few arrests. Donnie has brought his motorcycle helmet, bright yellow like a target. He always brings it to demonstrations, tucking his long hair into it and fastening the chin strap just as an event gets started. Only this time I talk Donnie into letting Sam wear it. Sam doesn't want to but I tell him he has to.

"What for?"

"Because Mom will kill me if you get clubbed in the head."

The one I worry about is Karl. He is so tall and his head sticks out above the crowd, an obvious and tempting target. Karl wanders through the heart of the police line unafraid, without ever flinching or covering up, tear gas swirling below his high head.

This is how we were spending weekends. But I have to get Sam out of here and Karl, a foreigner on a tourist visa, comes with me. Surprisingly, it is Sam who points out to Karl that as a foreigner he could not afford to get arrested. Rachel insists on staying longer, on "not backing off from the pigs," and Donnie stays with her while we go back to the little café and wait. Sam, red-eyed, his cheeks wet with tears, has had a moving experience. I knew he would. He is now talking revolution with Karl, who enthusiastically says to him, "A revolution does not fall when it's ripe. You have to pick it." It is not difficult to guess the source of these words of inspiration.

They are now engaged in an improbable conversation about New England–West Berlin solidarity. But what I am thinking is that Fenway Park is only about two blocks away and the Red Sox are playing the Yankees. Jim Lonborg, a great right-hander, is starting for the Sox against Mel Stottlemyre, who is also having a great year. Karl, remembering baseball from his brief American childhood, thinks going to the game is a great idea. Sam questions, "Is it right to go to a baseball game after a demonstration?"

Karl smiles, cocks his beret appropriately askew, and says, "One must harden without ever losing tenderness." Sam wonders what that means while I wonder if there is any occasion for which Karl cannot find a Che Guevara quote.

When Rachel and Donnie arrive Rachel has no enthusiasm for the plan. But Donnie wants to go. I know what he is thinking because I am having the same thought: Stanley should be here. The last time I went to Fenway Park was with Donnie and Stanley, right after our high school graduation. That was also a Yankees game. Stanley and I liked to harass Donnie about his rooting for the Yankees. Rachel looks like she is about to cry and I almost back down, but then I realize that her red eyes only have that look from the tear gas. She decides to come along, maybe because my eyes have the same look or maybe because young Che, the German revolutionary, is smiling so eagerly, nodding his head with such excitement—and looking so goofy.

We buy the cheapest seats we can, high above right field. I have never understood why these seats are cheap. The batter is a long way away, but it is the lowest outfield wall so it is a good place to catch home run balls. Sam, Dad, and I used to go there with gloves hoping to catch a home run ball hit into the stands, though we never did. Sam and I explain this to Karl and he seems very excited. We point out the red seat only four rows behind us where Ted Williams hit a home run in 1946, the longest bomb ever hit out of Fenway Park. I tell Karl how it hit a man in that seat on the head, crashing through his straw hat. Karl looks very impressed.

I can see that Karl, in his excitement, does not remember much about baseball because he is shouting something about a touchdown. The Yankees are leading for the entire game. Only Donnie, clutching his motorcycle helmet in his lap, is happy. The Yankees are two runs ahead in the seventh inning when the Red Sox get two singles and Carl Yastrzemski comes to bat. On the third pitch he sends the ball over the diamond, past the outfield, and right at us. While everyone around us strains to catch the ball, Karl, who has no fear of club-wielding police but remembers the poor man in the straw hat, folds up his long body, curling into the space in front of his seat, and covers his head, shouting, "Touch*d-o-w-n-n-n*," holding the last note.

The ball lands in Karl's seat with an enormous cracking sound that makes him look up. When he does, the ball bounces into his lap. Karl has Yaz's home run ball. That is all it takes to turn the three of us into little boys again. Donnie and I argue about what kind of pitch Yaz hit. Donnie insists that between Mantle and Joe Pepitone the Yankees will come back.

"Yeah, you always think that, but they're through," I say.

Rachel is listening with quiet disdain. After the Red Sox win, Sam says to Karl—who is studying his souvenir—"You've got to get Yaz to sign it, man!" Over Rachel's protests we elbow our way into the crowd in narrow Yawkey Way and wait for Yastrzemski to come out. By then the crowd is smaller and we manage to get up to him. The ballplayer, a head shorter than Karl, looks surprisingly small. Karl is so excited to talk to him that his English fails him. He says, "*Meine Nom* is Karl too and I am from Germany. I caught dis from your touchdown."

"He means home run," Sam shouts anxiously.

"*Jah*, could you sign it 'From Carl to Karl'?"

"Sure," Yaz says with a big smile. As he writes on the ball, Sam, who knows the value of a good souvenir, shouts, "But don't forget to add 'Yastrzemski.'"

He reclicks his pen and adds his last name.

What a night. I could stay up talking to Karl until dawn. But Rachel points out that we have to get Sam back. Our parents are probably worried.

Karl (Moltke, not Yastrzemski) and I swear we will stay in touch, but for some reason I think we probably won't. We hug and then touch fists, and he says, "Friends and brothers in the revolution." If I read about West Berlin exploding and Germany in flames, I will know that at the center of it will be a radical revolutionary with a home run ball signed by Carl Yastrzemski.

CHAPTER TWENTY-ONE
OUR FIRST TRIP
TO AMERICA

We are all back in Haley for the summer and when Rachel comes for a visit, I introduce her to Rocco. We talk about his problem and Rachel tells us she knows a draft counselor in Boston. Rocco goes to talk with him and discovers that because his father died in combat in Korea, he will not be drafted. So he signs with the Detroit Tigers and is sent to a class-B team called the Warsaw Warriors. When Stanley hears that they sent him to pitch for a team in Warsaw, he laughs, since his family left Warsaw and never had anything good to say about it. But this turns out to be Warsaw, Indiana, in a midwestern league called the Triple I—Illinois, Indiana, Iowa.

Donnie comes up with the idea of us all going to Warsaw to see Rocco play. Donnie has a big blue van, a Ford Econoline. He has taken out the back seats and put in two beds and calls the van "the love machine." He points out that with the love machine we have no need for the expense of motels and we can get there quickly by driving and sleeping in shifts. We have little money, and what we do have we are saving for college. We also have little time because our summer jobs are about to start. Stanley is working at the tool-and-die plant. Donnie is working in the front office of a textile company. And I have been hired to spend my summer in the cool comfort of a large, dark walk-in refrigerator, keeping the shelves of the dairy store stocked.

Stanley comes up with the idea that during the trip we can live on canned food, and he puts a case of Campbell's Pork and Beans in the van. So I contribute some cans of tuna and Donnie brings cans of soup. Now with the Cold War getting hotter we are all eating from our family shelters.

We leave Haley and only get as far as Connecticut when Stanley hungers for some pork and beans. Then we remember that no one thought to bring a can opener and we have to stop in a store to buy one. This keeps us laughing until New Jersey. At eighty miles an hour on the wide lanes of the

Pennsylvania Turnpike we are singing Motown—the Four Tops, Smokey Robinson, and Martha Reeves. We take turns driving and sleeping. Cold canned food tastes a lot better than you might think and soon we are in Warsaw, Indiana.

This is a different place and we are foreigners. It reminds me of being at sea on a calm day, but there is no water. It is just so flat, the horizon is always straight ahead, and the houses and even the people stick out against a too-bright blue sky. Maybe that is why the girls all dress in bright colors—no browns or grays, only true red, blue, or yellow. The men, even the ones our age, wear short-sleeved white shirts and have haircuts like Dickey Panicelli's when he got back from boot camp.

We don't fit in. Our hair is longer, especially Donnie's. He has a beard, I have a mustache, and Stanley has a lot of facial hairs though they don't seem to add up to much. We're still wearing our World War II clothes—Stanley in his Eisenhower jacket and me in my uncle's field jacket.

Though nobody says so, they don't like us. They grumble a lot about hippies, college students, and draft dodgers—which are all the same thing in their minds and they think that's what we are. And, of course, they are right. Several times, police order our van to pull over. They study us and ask what we are doing in Warsaw. Everything changes when we tell them that we have a friend on the Warriors. Then we all talk baseball.

But we don't really speak the same language. They have a twang, though a policeman, whom we were getting along with, became very angry when Stanley asked him why he spoke with a southern accent. They have trouble understanding us too. They say we have a "Kennedy accent," which isn't true and clearly they don't mean it as a compliment. At the baseball stadium we ask an attendant where to park and he says contemptuously, "What do you mean, 'puk'?" But then I realize that he really doesn't understand what we are asking.

The home of the Warsaw Warriors is no larger or in any way better than the ball fields we played on in high school. But the players are. The catcher knows how to catch Rocco's hard fastball and guides him, and he is getting more control, looking better than I ever saw him in Haley. They only let him throw about ten pitches a day, which is good for us because it means we get to see him play all three days we are there. And we can see from the attention the manager and coaches give him that he is being seen as a serious prospect. He seems very happy to see us in this town where everyone speaks differently and where he is the only short dark person with thick curly black hair. He is in training and refuses to eat canned food and makes us go to this local restaurant that is so cheap we wonder why we have been eating canned food.

The only women in the restaurant are waitresses. The customers are all men and they are mostly talking about "the Negroes." Sometimes they use less polite words. They are very angry about "the Negroes." There have been race riots in Cleveland and a few other cities, and the men of Warsaw have strong ideas about what to do in Warsaw when "the Negroes" start rioting. This seems odd because, as far as I can tell, there are no Negroes, not even at the baseball games.

They also talk about the war and how we are winning in spite of the hippies. We eat very quietly. Probably the only reason they let us in is that we are with a baseball player.

At the baseball game we sit next to a group of men who are talking very loudly about "the Negroes." Then they leave, all but one. He looks about our age and is very tall with enormous ears—or does the haircut just make it look that way? I can't help myself. I have to ask someone.

"I notice everyone here is talking about the Negroes coming. Who is coming?"

He smiles and slowly looks around and then laughs. "Damned if I know. I keep asking my dad the same question."

He introduces himself as Lester Parkman and I say, "Joel Bloom." We shake hands. My hand hurts from his grip.

"You fellows aren't from here," Lester says.

"No, Massachusetts."

"Damn," he says, seeming genuinely excited. "That's why you have those Kennedy accents." Then he moves his face closer to mine, staring. "You Jew?" asks Lester.

Is he saying "You Jew, you," or is he really asking? Stanley is looking very worried. I say that I am and his face lights up. "Damn! I've never seen a Jew before. You fellows too?" he says to Stanley and Donnie. When they shake their heads he looks disappointed.

Lester has volunteered to be a marine infantryman. He is leaving in four days. As I talk to him I realize he is not that different from me. He doesn't know where Vietnam is and he doesn't want to go. "I don't have anything against Vietnamese people. I don't even know what they want," Lester says. "I guess they just want people to stop invading their country."

"So if you feel that way, how can you go kill them?"

Lester shrugs. "No choice. I'm not going to be a draft dodger." When Lester gets out of the marines he wants to go to college, and he hopes to eventually be the principal of the high school in Warsaw. For two days we go to ball games and little restaurants and walk around town and talk and talk. He keeps saying that he doesn't want to kill Vietnamese but he has no choice. I cannot convince him that he does have a choice. And under his terms he doesn't, because he knows that if he doesn't go to Vietnam he will never be the principal of the Warsaw high school.

The last time I see him we hug. I wish him good luck and he wishes me good luck, which reminds me that I haven't figured this out either, I have just deferred the decision by going to college. I hug Rocco too and tell him next time I watch him play it will be on a class-A team, and he smiles and pats my shoulder so hard it hurts.

In the van again, on canned food again, singing more Motown, we talk all the way back about baseball and Rocco and Lester. I feel like it would be very hard to stop a war in this country. No matter what you did in New England, there would always be Indiana. But the truth is, as Stanley glumly says, "Lester isn't any different from us."

CHAPTER TWENTY-TWO
IT'S NOT THAT EASY

He is beautiful, my new roommate. Donnie LePine talked me into getting an apartment with him. It is in a small building on the edge of town. Donnie is resplendent in his long locks. But it doesn't come easy, and I see hours of shampooing, brushing, setting it in a stocking cap. Rachel, who spends no time at all on her hair, is more beautiful.

There are other people living in the apartment. There is someone sleeping on our couch right now. His boots are on the couch and he is snoring but I have no idea who he is or who most of the people here are.

Influenced by one of the most famous professors at Whiting, Henry B. Moreland, I have decided to major in biology. Moreland is the author of a dozen books on Darwin and the natural order. He is also an outspoken presence at antiwar marches in Washington and around the country. He is one of the celebrity marchers—well-known writers, lawyers, and scientists who are always seen at the heads of the marches. The police seem to avoid clubbing that front row though I am sure Moreland has inhaled his share of tear gas.

My favorite Moreland moment was during a lecture when a student in an Air Force ROTC uniform challenged him.

"Professor Moreland, would you say that violence is natural?"

Moreland squinted through his thick-lensed glasses and pushed his long gray hair off his forehead. "Well, that would depend on the act. But I would say that the tendency to react with violence is common in nature. Most animals, including human beings, are built with an instinct for violence as a survival mechanism."

"Then," said the young recruit, certain that he had the old professor, "war is a natural thing. It is what we are built to do. What we are supposed to be doing."

The hall was completely silent, waiting for Moreland's answer. "War may be caused by biological impulses, but impulses being biological does not make them natural and it does not make them right. We have biological impulses to be naked and eat with our fingers. That doesn't mean anyone wants to see you like that."

The class broke into loud laughter. In some ways this was a fun time to be going to college. In other ways it was not.

The war goes on and that is what we are all talking about most of the time. Walter Cronkite, that same distinctive voice from the evening news who explained World War II to me in my childhood, is on television every night reporting on the deaths, the killings, the ever-larger numbers of troops being called up. Almost twenty thousand Americans and maybe a million Vietnamese have been killed. The generals think that if we kill enough of them the Vietnamese will give up, but that isn't happening.

We seem helpless to stop this killing. We don't want to be like the Germans we learned about as children. We want to speak out. We want to do something. We have constant demonstrations. They are all over the country. The crowds keep getting bigger. But it doesn't do anything except maybe make the police, Rachel's "pigs," even crazier. They are becoming more violent with every march.

Donnie and I still talk about Lester. He must be a marine by now. We wonder if he is in Vietnam, if we are about to see him on television, if he will survive to be a principal. "It's the Lesters of the country that we have to organize," says Donnie.

"I don't think you can," I say. "Until they get back. Then they will be ready."

"Then you have the base of a real revolution," says Rachel. "Organize the veterans. That's how the Bolsheviks won."

✕ ✕ ✕

Home for a visit I find that Popeye Panicelli angrily approves of the beating of demonstrators. I wonder if he understands that I am one of them. He says, "Those kids get what they deserve." And I guess a lot of the police feel that way. Dickey served, so why don't I? But then Dickey, who always gets attention when he speaks because he hardly ever does anymore, says, "And we're getting what we deserve in Vietnam."

Popeye doesn't answer. I don't think they talk to each other much. At night I can still hear Dickey screaming.

✕ ✕ ✕

There are a lot of draft counselors. They are mostly just kids like me. Sometimes they are parents of kids like me. They don't know that much about the draft but they meet with someone who gives them information and then they go to the poor parts of cities and work as counselors. I don't want to do that. But I do keep thinking about Dickey. Suppose I had tried to talk him out of going. Suppose I had convinced him. Wouldn't that have been a good thing to do? But why would I have had any more luck with him than I had with Lester?

Still, I want to start trying to talk guys out of it, so I go see Rachel's friend Myron, in Boston, the one who helped Rocco. He is in a storefront on Blue Hill Avenue in Dorchester, the widest street in a three-story neighborhood. It used to be a Jewish neighborhood but now it is black. Myron is one of the last Jews. His office is next to the Black Panthers' office. These Panthers are as beautiful as Donnie. They dress in black with black berets on their heads.

Myron, on the other hand, is in blue—blue jeans, blue work shirt, and, for contrast, a string of red beads. His office, called "The Draft Project," is an empty room except for five folding chairs. The walls are covered with posters, mostly against the war but also supporting the United Farm Workers, a California-Mexican group calling for the boycott of grapes. I am not sure why we should be boycotting grapes but I think we should all support each other's causes, so I resolve to eat no more grapes—though I wasn't eating them very much before.

"There is always a choice," says Myron. "You can refuse the draft on moral grounds. They will give you a hearing. If you lose, your choices are to go to jail or to Canada." Myron is very concise about this, like a professor laying out the semester's curriculum. "Those are your options," he says.

But they are not my options. They are the options of the guys I want to talk to. I talk to kids who aren't going to college about not going into the army. I tell them they can refuse or find a way out. But they go in anyway. Sometimes about a year later they come back looking different and they track me down just to say "You were right." That's what Dickey would have said too. But so far I haven't talked anyone out of going.

It occurs to me that maybe there were a lot of Germans who wanted to stop the Nazis. Maybe they couldn't figure out what to do. But no one would accept that excuse from them afterward.

At our apartment my roommates are trying to figure out what to do. "We have to bring the war home so the average American is paying, so he feels it," Donnie keeps saying.

"Doesn't he feel it now?" I ask.

"Apparently not," says Donnie. "He needs to bleed some. We need more blood on the streets."

The odd thing is that while Donnie is saying these things he is always shampooing or brushing or setting his shining hair. There is this one small kid who's been staying in the apartment, with wire-rimmed glasses, the kind Benjamin Franklin wore. There are always kids staying here that I don't know. For a while there was Tubs, who played a clarinet and was very funny. You have to like a fat man who calls himself Tubs. I never learned his real name. Then there was Wet Wendy. I suppose her name really was Wendy. We called her Wet Wendy because she was constantly taking showers and her hair was always wet. We were all glad when she left because it freed up the bathroom. Now there is this guy. I don't know his name or if he is a Whiting student or anything about him, but he is always here and he never says a word. No matter what anyone proposes, no matter how wild or violent or dangerous, he nods his head eagerly in agreement.

I think he must be an informer. He probably works for the FBI. If I am right, this is bad news for Rachel because she is always making comments about the "pigs" and what we ought to do to get back at them. If this is getting reported to the FBI, they will find a way to get her. I have told her this and she laughs and says, "Not if we get them first."

I find it hard to talk to Rachel these days. I don't think we see things in the same way. Meanwhile, every time I call home my mother always asks, "How is that nice girl Rachel?"

Donnie and Rachel and some others have come up with

this crazy idea about a bomb that would make a lot of noise but not hurt anyone. But I wonder, "If we get into this business of bombing, how are we better than the generals?"

"Because," Donnie says, lifting off a knit cap like an unveiling, his newly conditioned hair flowing down into view, "our bomb won't hurt anyone."

"Maybe we *should* hurt someone," says Rachel.

After a moment of silence punctuated by the mute kid in the glasses excitedly nodding his head, Donnie says, "How does it look? I used this new herbal rinse. It's a recipe from a Pueblo Indian group. The recipe is from before Columbus."

The kid in the wire-rimmed glasses continues his eager nodding.

I have other ideas. John Kennedy's brother Robert is running for president. It's funny—when John Kennedy was president, I was the least enthusiastic Kennedy kid in Massachusetts. But I have a lot of hopes for the brother. Sam is already working for him. He is only a high school junior but he has gone to the Kennedy headquarters in New York as part of a youth movement and has even met Kennedy. They say Robert is the most serious of the Kennedys, so that is perfect for Sam. I think Kennedy will stop the war and I think he knows how to get elected, and I resolve that I will work for his campaign. And then the war will end at last. Donnie doesn't say anything because we always have this sadness between us about the name "Kennedy." But Rachel wants no part of this Kennedy campaign. "I want revolution, not another President Kennedy."

The kid in the wire-rimmed glasses nods in agreement.

CHAPTER TWENTY-THREE
THE BOMB

Throughout my sophomore year the bad times keep getting worse. Martin Luther King Jr. was killed yesterday. How could something be so shocking without being at all surprising? Everyone always thought he might be killed. He did too. He talked about dying young all the time. He spoke about it just the day before he was shot. Even when we were kids in Haley this had been a topic. Some said he deserved to die. Well, only Tony Scaratini. But we grew up with Martin Luther King Jr. He was always there, never tiring, fighting towns, states, the government—demanding change. At our college he had grown out of fashion. Both black and white kids are listening to more radical black leaders who laugh at the peaceful ways of the civil rights movement. They preach revolution and call for violence. They don't believe that big shows like demonstrations accomplish anything. And I have to wonder about it myself. Young blacks are calling for "direct action," the same kind of thing Rachel and Donnie talk about for stopping the war. Now King is gone and in our apartment everyone is crying—except the kid with the wire-rimmed glasses, who just sits there looking like he is waiting for us to stop. But even Rachel, who always said King was too soft and just not the stuff of revolution, has so many tears running down her face that the top of her white shirt is getting wet.

✕ ✕ ✕

Immediately after King's death it seems that everyone gets a little harder, a little meaner. We organize a demonstration on campus. It is not a large university so we do not expect too large a crowd. But about twenty thousand people show up. It is going well, peacefully, and the police are staying on the sidelines. They have shields, those clear plastic ones that look like motorcycle windshields, and they all wear blue helmets, though I don't know why. What are they worried about? We are unarmed and peaceful. Maybe it is an example of judging others by yourself.

Suddenly black vans are arriving—three . . . no, four . . . no, five. Out of them come helmeted men wearing strange padding and tugging on the leashes of large snarling black-backed German shepherds.

The dogs are now running through the crowd lunging at demonstrators. It looks like they are going for their throats but I am not sure. When they jump on demonstrators they knock them down and somehow hold them. Two policemen with dogs still on leashes are heading straight for Rachel. I run toward her though I have no idea what I am going to do. The first dog is released—a burly athletic animal that leaps up and knocks her over.

I would not believe this if I didn't see it. One of the policemen rears back, almost in a batter's stance, swings his club, and hits Rachel so hard on the head that even though I am still ten feet away I hear the melon-like thud of the club hitting her head. Her head snaps to the side in an unnatural movement. The police take their dogs and go off to the next victim. They've killed Rachel!

When I reach her, her face is white and there is blood streaming from her forehead, but she is still breathing. She opens her eyes, faintly smiles, and says something I can't hear. But I know what she's saying—"Pigs."

✕ ✕ ✕

"Let's get her to the hospital, man," says a voice over my shoulder. It's Donnie, and as I look past him I see that we are the only ones left on the campus mall. There are no demonstrators, no other injured people, no police, and no dogs.

"Everyone's gone," I say.

Donnie shrugs.

"You would think there would be some reporters or something."

Donnie looks around and shrugs again.

"So they are just going to get away with it," says Rachel, holding her head. "No one will know what they did."

"Let's get her to the hospital."

"Wait," says Rachel. "Suppose two hundred kids turn up wounded at the hospital. That will get some attention."

"Yes, but there's only you," says Donnie.

"But we could get a lot more," I hear myself say.

So we have hatched a plot. I will run ahead with Rachel to the hospital and Donnie will get as many students as he can find and have them come to the hospital complaining of being beaten up, and then some newspeople will come.

At the hospital the nurse asks Rachel what happened and she tells her that the police beat her up at a demonstration and everyone seems satisfied with that explanation. There are no more questions. They run some tests. She is fine. No concussion, no need for stitches. We try to stall longer, but no one comes, so we leave.

✕ ✕ ✕

Now I am ready to strike back. It is a beautiful spring, with warm sunny days and evenings of soft rain that make things bloom and grow. But I am angry. We all are. What have these demonstrations accomplished? The killing goes on and on. We are having a meeting in the apartment. My only condition is that we don't physically hurt anyone. When I think about the reality that in a year or two I could be in Vietnam, I find it hard to believe that I would actually kill people. I can imagine being in the military, being in a war. I have imagined it all my life. But I can't imagine killing Vietnamese people. More to the point, I can't imagine how I will live with myself after I do. So I am not about to kill anyone here to try to stop the killing there. I don't even want to hit the man who beat Rachel. I don't want to be like him. But I also don't want the incident to go unnoticed. So we come up with another plan.

Close to town there is a statue of Thomas Pickering, who captured a nearby fort from the British in the Revolutionary War. No one guards this statue or even looks at it. Probably the one exception to that is a trustee of the college, C. Bradford Harrington, whom no one has ever seen but who claims to be a direct descendant of Thomas Pickering. Why would anyone lie about that? His family had the statue built. There are two extraordinary things about this statue that were pointed out to us by Donnie LePine. (The one consistent thing about Donnie in all the years I have known him is that he always does his homework.)

The first extraordinary thing is that, although it is a bronze statue, it stands on a wooden base. The second is that the statue is on the edge of town next to a thick pine woods. Why are these two things significant? Because none of us knows how to make a bomb. I try to remember all the explosive elements from Mr. Shaker's chemistry class and how to make something with nitrogen. In a world of volatile elements and unstable compounds it should be easy, but I don't know how to do it. Donnie, who was not interested in chemistry, claims to know how to make a Molotov cocktail. He learned this from a movie about anti-Nazi partisans in the mountains somewhere. By coincidence the movie, which I watched with my uncle, is set in a pine forest that looks a lot like the area behind the Pickering statue. A Molotov cocktail won't blow up the statue but it could burn down the wooden base.

The importance of the woods is that we could cut through the trees, throw the bomb, and disappear back into the woods—and no one would see us. We have a

cardboard sign that we will leave near the statue: THIS FIRE
WAS SET TO PROTEST THE CAMPUS MASSACRE OF MAY 29.
Then the press will scramble to find out what the campus
massacre on May 29 was. We make the sign by cutting ran-
dom letters from magazines so there is no handwriting clue
left. We learned how to do that from a movie about a kid-
napping, starring Glenn Ford.

A Molotov cocktail, according to Donnie, is just a bottle
filled with rocks and gasoline and stopped up with some
rolled cloth as a wick. We have made two because we had
two large bottles, both from wine. We considered making a
third with a ketchup bottle but decided it was too small.
Two will be fine. There are five of us in the apartment and
we draw straws for who will go. The short straws win.

Naturally, Donnie draws one of the short straws because
he always wins. Back in Haley he never even lost a coin
toss. I have the other short straw. Donnie disappears into
his bedroom and comes out a few minutes later and says,
"All set."

I look up in wonder. Donnie is wearing a revolutionary
guerrilla fighter outfit. He has on black boots, tight black
jeans, a black turtleneck sweater, and a black knit hat.

I guess I am staring because he explains, "Harder to see
you in the dark."

That's probably true. Has he done this before?

He looks great! I am wearing these stupid brown loafers that I haven't worn since Haley. I have boots, but they chose today for a heel to come off. I am wearing jeans, a blue shirt, and my Battle of the Bulge fatigues jacket, which now comes down barely below my waist because I have grown taller than my uncle.

Rachel is driving us, with another kid named Trotsky—probably not his real name (it wasn't even the real Trotsky's real name) but it's what everyone calls him. He claims to have a radical edge on all of us because he dropped out of Brandeis. Brandeis is a university near Boston but I do not know if his superior credentials as a radical are supposed to come from his having gone there or from having dropped out. Not many kids drop out of school these days because of the draft. But Trotsky isn't being drafted, maybe because he is too fat. If you can be too fat for the military, Trotsky would qualify.

It is a dark moonless night and Rachel and Trotsky are dropping us off at the far edge of the woods. The woods will be our cover and no one will see us go in or out. Rachel is driving us in her Mao-mobile. We did realize that a bright red Volkswagen might be conspicuous but Donnie had painted flowers all over his van, which seemed even easier to notice. We get out of the car. I have one bottle. Donnie has the other. I have the sign. Rachel and Trotsky have promised to periodically check back on us so that they can pick us up and the police won't spot us suspiciously walking around. Suddenly it occurs to me that Donnie's outfit may not be a good idea. Why advertise? If you were robbing a bank, would you wear a bank robber outfit?

The car is about to leave when I remember something.

"Wait!"

The car jerks to a stop. Everyone is looking at me. Sheepishly I grin. "Anybody have matches?"

Trotsky and Rachel fumble around and Donnie finds some in the glove compartment. He puts them in a pocket and we are off to attack Pickering.

Donnie stops just as we are entering the woods. Even in the dark I can see his wide smile. "Off to war together at last, Aramis."

"Athos," I say, and we embrace.

"Hey, Joel," says Donnie, his hands still on my shoulders, "remember the green stones?"

"Jade."

"Montana jade." We both laugh and then he asks, "Do you still have yours?"

"I don't know. Maybe at my parents' house somewhere. You?"

"Same. Maybe at my parents'. What do you want to bet Stanley still has his right in his pocket." We laugh again and turn in to the woods.

It is very dark in the woods. I take about three careful steps and then there is a sucking noise. I pull up my right foot and there is no brown loafer on it. I cannot see anything. Now I am wondering why we didn't think to bring a flashlight. I could light a match, but the matches are critical and I shouldn't waste them. I cannot find the shoe.

I decide to hobble on. Donnie was right about his outfit. I cannot see him and I keep calling to him to find out where he is. Sometimes his voice is in front of me, sometimes behind me.

After about an hour, maybe longer, I start to think that these woods are a lot bigger than I had thought. Strange, because New Hampshire's not that big. Now I hear an odd sound from Donnie. He has tripped over a rock and can't find his bomb. We grope around but can't feel it. We consider lighting a match but then remember that matches are not a good way to hunt for gasoline bombs. We decide to leave it. One will be enough. We hope.

I think it has been another hour now and I smell a lot of gasoline and think maybe some of it has spilled on my jeans. I would like to see, because if there is no more gas in the bottle there is no point in going on. The sign has fallen in the mud a few times and I am not sure it is readable. Maybe we should check on that. Actually I can almost read the sign because the lettering is against a white background. Maybe Donnie could stand away from me and the gasoline, and light a match. He takes the sign and walks ahead about six feet through the trees. I can see him clearly now. My eyes must be adjusting.

Then I realize that I am seeing better because it is dawn.

"If we wait a little longer it will be daylight and we can find our way back to the road."

"Or we can just go into town. Even if we do look strange, we didn't do anything. Nothing has happened. So we can just walk through town," Donnie points out.

We leave the second bottle in the woods and fold up the sign. There is nothing to hide. Donnie is right. And I feel a little relieved about that. My days as a revolutionary guerrilla fighter are over. Soon there is enough light for us to find our way into town. It is not far away although in a completely different direction from where we had been heading. On the way back to the apartment, Rachel, who has been circling town all night, pulls up next to us. Nobody noticed the red Volkswagen driving around. But why should they, since nothing has happened? We give her the disappointing news. For some reason, she just laughs. Then we all laugh. Not knowing what to do, Trotsky laughs too.

✕ ✕ ✕

Ex-guerrillas, we are studying for our final exams. I take a break and turn on the television but I doze. I can hear they are running some old film of the Kennedy assassination. Suddenly I realize it is *this* Kennedy, the brother. They have killed Bobby too. Donnie walks into the room and I start to tell him but realize I can't tell him about another Kennedy assassination. So I say nothing and he sees it on television.

Rachel is right, I understand that now. You can't change things if every time someone tries, he is killed. Maybe my thinking is completely wrong and I am not recognizing the way the world really is. Maybe, like Martin Luther King, I am too soft. And isn't that just another way of not standing up, of being the German?

I call Sam, thinking how upset he will be too. He is upset, but he is not thinking the way I am. He is talking politics. He is worried about the Kennedy delegates. Do they give them to McCarthy or to a new antiwar candidate? How do they stop Humphrey . . .

I let him talk but I am not listening. It doesn't matter to me because no one who will stop the war is going to get the nomination. And if someone could, he would just be shot.

The war is still on.

CHAPTER TWENTY-FOUR
INDUCTION

To me, Bobby Kennedy's death was the final death of wounded hope. I finished my last two years of college without believing there was anything much anyone could do. I studied biology and tried to understand why the world is arranged the way it is. Professor Moreland urged us to study Darwin and promised that if we understood the natural order we could understand ourselves. Like Moreland and most everyone else I know, I go to demonstrations but I realize they won't stop the war. Nixon, whom I thought I had left behind in my childhood, is now president. Was this what Darwin meant by the survival of the fittest? At this rate we will be back to Eisenhower soon.

But, bad as the world is, I don't want to make it any worse. My college education, my draft deferment, has slipped by. Still, I know that no matter what happens, I will not be killing Vietnamese people for Richard Nixon or anyone else. In my mind I keep reviewing the alternatives as presented by Myron in Dorchester.

But now there is another possibility. Now there is a lottery in which a number will be assigned to every day of the year. If your birthday has a high number you are probably free. If you have a low number you will almost certainly be going into the military. Donnie LePine, for whom everything always turns out well, draws number 347 and he is out of the draft. The only surprise is that he didn't get number 365. Donnie has decided to drop out of school for a while and "work for the movement."

December 7, my birthday, pulls number twelve. My low number isn't surprising to me. It is becoming clearer every day that this war is my destiny. I will have to face it—fight it or refuse to fight it. But I will not just get out of it by something as easy as a lottery number.

✕ ✕ ✕

I am officially no longer a student. I am twenty-one years old and I have just finished my last final exam. What this means to me is that my draft deferment has ended and I am eligible.

Detroit has faded since it won the 1968 World Series. They didn't do well last year. This year their star pitcher, Denny McLain, was suspended for carrying a gun when traveling with the team. The world is so mad that you don't even ask why he wanted to carry a gun. It was not allowed and he was suspended for half the season. I only care because they are now short a pitcher and so maybe they are going to bring up a rookie left-hander named Pizzutti. The last I heard from Rocco, he had made Double A. Donnie and Stanley and I always said we would go see him play again but we never have. Now Donnie is off with his high lottery number working for the movement. I think he is in hiding, or as he and Rachel would say, "gone underground." Stanley and I, with low lottery numbers, are coming out of college about to face induction into the military. Isn't this the reverse of what should happen? Shouldn't Stanley and I be the ones to go into hiding? At least Rocco has beaten the draft.

After finishing the exam, I return to my apartment where I plan to call my parents to explain that there is nothing to celebrate and that I do not want to attend my graduation. But as soon as I get there, the telephone starts ringing. The way I am feeling, I half expect it to be the army telling me to report for duty.

Close. It is my father telling me my draft notice has arrived. It is as if the military had been watching. I am almost surprised that they mailed the notice to my parents' home rather than have someone outside the test room waiting for me.

I think I should just refuse to go. That would be better than going and then refusing to fight. My father has a friend who can get me into the Army Reserve and then I wouldn't have to go to Vietnam. But that would still be supporting the war, not resisting it. If you participate in the military in any way, you are participating in the war. The fact that I might manage to get an easier job for myself would not be opposing the war.

Rachel says I should go in and "work for the movement" from within the army. According to her, I should try to get soldiers to rebel. Isn't that how revolutions begin? Someone else tells me I should just tell the army that this is my plan, and then they won't take me. Stanley insists that he has spoken to medical students and knows how to get medically rejected. But I don't have anything wrong with me.

My parents are angry that I won't go into the reserves. "You're just being stubborn," my mother says. I argue that it is more complicated than that.

My father insists, "There's a right way and a wrong way to do these things. You can go into the reserves and stay away from the war and it will at least be *legal*. Once you do things that are not legal, you don't stand for anything. You're just a criminal. You could go to jail."

"I know that."

But finally he gives me his blessing down in the shelter, tuna in hand. He says, "I think it's good to try for this exemption on moral grounds, as long as you accept that after you lose you will go in."

This did not make any sense but he was happy with it so I didn't argue.

My uncle cannot believe that anyone would just refuse to serve. He cannot even talk about it. I think he does not like the idea that he had a choice. The idea that war is "doing what you have to do" is very important to him.

I am sitting on the swing in the backyard, the old battlefield where Donnie and Stanley and I formed our brotherhood. I wonder what happened to the Nazi hats and canteens and Stanley's flag of surrender. Sam comes out with his slow bearlike walk. I can see he has something on his mind. He always does. All he says is, "Hi, Joel."

"Hi, Sam."

There is a long silence while Sam prepares what he wants to say and I wait for it.

"Joel? The Army Reserve is a good spot. This is an out-fit that will never be called up."

"I thought you were against the war?"

"I am but . . . this will ruin your whole future."

"It will just shape it in a different way. I have no idea what my future is. But it is not killing Vietnamese people."

There is another long silence except that the crickets in the yard are very loud. Warm summer nights, the chirp of crickets—I keep remembering those summers with nothing to do but play war and baseball.

"Joel, if you do this it will ruin *my* career. Joel, I want to go into politics."

He says this as though it is supposed to be surprising, but he has been in politics since he was in high school, and he is majoring in political science. Of course, so did Rachel and Donnie, but Sam is different.

"I'm going to work for Senator McGovern. He's going to run for president in 1972 and he'll stop the war. His staff has promised me a full-time job when I graduate but they are not going to want the brother of a draft dodger."

"Why? He opposes the war."

"That's why he can't afford to be surrounded by draft dodgers. He was a combat veteran."

So even George McGovern disapproves?

"It's just his staff looking out for him. It's not just that you'd be a draft dodger. You would be a felon. That would plague me my whole career."

I can't help but think the whole reason Sam is planning out his career is that he got such a high lottery number he doesn't even have to think about the draft. I think about Lester. Sam has put me in Lester's shoes. If I don't go it will ruin a career, although in my case it's not even *my* career. I don't like the idea of Sam being plagued his whole life by a decision I made. But to ignore what is right because it will be hard for your family—isn't that being the German? Wasn't that one of the standard excuses? Can I kill Vietnamese people because it would look best for my brother's career?

The only one who approves of my decision to outright refuse is Dickey Panicelli. He walks up to the fence between our yards and stares over at me, or into the night darkness, in silence, and after a few minutes says, "I wish to hell I had taken five fucking minutes to sit on a swing and think before I signed up. I bet I wouldn't have done it."

x x x

I am to report to South Station in Boston and go by train to the induction center. What a funny word "induction" is. It sounds like being sucked into some kind of duct. We are all here to be inducted.

Stanley is here too. He is sick because he has eaten ninety-two eggs in an attempt to raise his albumen count. No one knows exactly what albumen is, but it is in eggs and everyone says they won't take you if you have too much of it. Looking at Stanley you would think too much albumen turns you green, but maybe that's just the effect of too many eggs.

Brian Sorenstag is talking with a ridiculous lisp that makes him sound like Elmer Fudd. He is hoping to convince the army that he is gay, though the gay people I know don't sound anything like Elmer Fudd. Was that cartoon supposed to be about a gay guy?

Everyone has something they are trying to do to get out. Everyone but Tony Scaratini. Tony stopped growing, so that he doesn't look any bigger than the rest of us now. He is even a little on the small side. For a moment I think maybe he stopped growing when I hit him back in high school. He is already losing his hair and has a humble, stoop-shouldered posture. He's very quiet and doesn't try to speak to any of us; none of us were ever interested in speaking to him. But we are fairly quiet anyway, thinking about the possibility of going to war or reviewing a strategy for not going or, in Stanley's case, feeling too sick to speak. But Brian Sorenstag is doing a lot of talking, practicing his Elmer Fudd accent.

Rocco and Donnie are the only ones missing. They have found their ways out.

It is a long and strange day of physical and psychological testing in a very large open space with rooms off to the side. Hundreds of men my age in various states of undress are being herded around by crisp humorless men in uniform. Being sheep is our introduction to military life. I try to fail everything but of course it doesn't work because that too is not my destiny. They show two squares and a circle and ask which one doesn't belong. Trying to sound earnest, I quickly respond, "Second square sir!"

A psychiatrist asks me if I have violent dreams. I say, "I think I am having one right now." But that just comes off as a joke. I guess it does not sound at all deranged. If you want to sound crazy you would have to say you love war. Dickey sounded a lot crazier to me when he went off to war than when he came back.

Anyone with a reasonable number of limbs, and, I suppose, the right albumen count, can pass this physical.

By the end of the day I am a big step closer to Vietnam. I have been found mentally, intellectually, and physically suitable for killing Vietnamese people. Shows what they know.

There are not many moments in life like this. This is the moment that everything in my life has led me to, the moment when I will finally face my war. And I know, without a twitch of hesitation, what to do. All day long a huge man in a khaki uniform, a sergeant, I think, has been shouting at us, sending us from station to station. He is a head taller than me, broad shouldered, and very fit-looking—probably a dangerous man to argue with. He has a red face and hair too short to guess at the color. Veins wander over his temples and you can see them pulsating when he shouts. He is exactly whom you would want for the crystallizing confrontation of your life.

I march up to him—as close to marching as I'm ever going to come—and I say, "Sir, I think this war is completely immoral and I refuse to participate in the military in any way."

He stares down at me. The whites of his eyes are crisscrossed with red veins, making his blue eyes look even bluer. Suddenly he looks to me like a man near the end of a long workday. He rolls those eyes and in a bored singsong recites, "Conscientious objector, line three."

CHAPTER TWENTY-FIVE
MY HEARING

Line three is very long but it is moving quickly. When I get to the front a civilian asks me if I wish to apply to be a conscientious objector. By law a person cannot be forced to fight if he believes it is morally wrong. The trick is to convince the military that you genuinely believe it is wrong. The military seems to find it hard to believe that people would really feel that way. In the short time it takes me to get from the back to the front of the line I become so convinced this is the right course for me that I am wondering what I have been agonizing over all these years.

I don't believe in the war and I will not kill anyone because to kill someone for a war you don't believe in would be a crime. I should just say so. If enough people said so it would be the end of the war. But though line three is long, it is not long enough to cause the war to stop. Looking around the induction center I see that they will still find enough new soldiers even without the people in line three. I am told that I can leave and that I will get a date for a hearing with my local draft board.

The old Haley gang gets on the train for the trip back. Each in his own way, we are all trying not to go to Vietnam, and though none of us has been rejected, we all have hearings pending to decide our cases—except for Stanley, who has another physical scheduled to check his albumen levels. This means eating another ninety-two eggs, making Stanley the least happy person on the train. We are all telling our stories and explaining our next moves and telling jokes about the big sergeant—except Tony Scaratini, who is sitting in silence. He is on his way back to Haley to say good-bye to his family. He has joined the army. He didn't even try to avoid it. We don't know if he wants to go, if he believes in the war. He doesn't say anything about it other than "They took me." There are a lot of jokes about how Tony is the perfect person to send, but I wonder what will happen to him.

✗ ✗ ✗

I am waiting for my hearing date on being a conscientious objector. The more I think about the phrase, the more it sounds right. I object because of my conscience. But I do not expect to win. I am either going to prison or to Canada. Canada seems better. I go to Dorchester and talk to Myron again and he says that you can only get recognized as a conscientious objector on religious grounds. That works with some religions, such as the Quakers. But given the violence of the Old Testament, it is not going to be easy to make the case that Judaism is a peaceful religion. Myron says, "You have to convince them that this is how you interpret Judaism."

To be honest, which I am told I can't be at my hearing, I have not spent a lot of time interpreting Judaism. But why do I think the way I do? It must have something to do with the way I was brought up. Any number of rabbis are available to help me prepare. These rabbis are all opposed to the war and want to help young men not go.

I plan to begin my argument at the hearing with a statement about how old and complicated the Jewish religion is and how it is accepted practice that different people take different things from it. To me the most important item is the sixth commandment: thou shall not kill. It is wrong and I will not do it.

I should stop right there. It's absolutely sincere and I should leave it at that. But everybody says I need more, and so I have worked out a long and scholarly treatise about

Abraham and the sacrifice of Isaac, and Jacob and Esau, and even casting the Maccabees in a bad light. If you don't know what I am talking about that is because I don't either. But I have worked out this talk with the rabbis and I hope the draft board will like it.

✗ ✗ ✗

This is my hearing. In a small room with one long table sit three men in herringbone sports jackets. Oddly, they all have on blue ties and white shirts. Is this a uniform? They look almost identical except one is losing his hair. He must be angry about that. He is clearly angry about something.

I am seated across from them. They are the teachers. I am the student, being judged, graded. I feel as though I have been given a detention before I even begin.

I open my lecture on the Jewish view of peace as expressed in the Old Testament. My argument sounds weak and they are just staring at me as if they are more interested in my clothes than in anything I am saying.

The more they stare, the harder I try, and the harder I try, the worse I am getting. I wish they would interrupt. Then the angry one does, saying, "So, you're Jewish?"

Has he not been listening to me at all?

I begin again. "I am, sir. And the Jewish religion has

taught me—" I am beginning all over again and fortunately he interrupts me.

"Would you fight the Nazis?"

I start thinking of Karl, the German exchange student. Then a second one joins in. "Just what would you do about World War II?"

The third one, looking interested for the first time, says, "You mean you wouldn't try to stop the Nazis?"

"I would," I say. "But there are different ways to do this." They aren't listening.

Nothing has changed over the course of my entire life. They still just want to talk about World War II, a discussion that continues until the hearing ends. Vietnam and the Vietnam War are never mentioned. I'll bet all three of them are World War II veterans. They just want to talk about their war. I think I would have opposed their war too. But that is not what I came prepared to talk about. I wanted to talk about *my* war.

There is nothing to do but wait for their letter.

PART THREE
MY LIFE

CHAPTER TWENTY-SIX
PLAYING DARTS

I got turned down for conscientious objector status and then turned down again on my appeal. All this took so long that by the time I am leaving for Canada, I hear Tony Scaratini is already done with boot camp and has been deployed to Vietnam.

I thought Rachel might drive me to Canada in her Mao-mobile. But she does not hesitate to show her disappointment that I haven't joined the military for the movement. Furthermore, she explains that she can't possibly cross the border because she is being watched by the government for her movement work. I am not sure at this point what that work is. I am no longer in her inner circle and I feel a reproach—she seems to feel that I can cross the border because I am so inconsequential. Our last meeting is a good-bye. It would have been good to have a girlfriend back in the States, coming to visit me, maybe even moving up with me. But there is no future for Rachel and me. I am going alone.

I ask Donnie to take me in his flowered van, a roomy transport to emigrate in. To my surprise he too complains of my running away instead of working for the movement from within the military.

"Why don't you do it?" I say.

"What do you mean?"

"I mean, just because you have a high lottery number doesn't stop you from volunteering."

He says nothing for a long minute and then says, "That is fantastic, Joel. That is exactly what I should do." He starts talking very rapidly about all his ideas for organizing within the military and I am wondering if I have just accidentally sent one of my oldest friends to Vietnam. Finally I say, "So, are you going to drive me to Canada?"

"No, man," he says. "I'm not going near that border. Come join the army with me."

"Donnie, I am not joining the army."

"Well, I'm not going to Canada with you."

"I was just asking for a ride."

✗ ✗ ✗

In the end Dickey drove me up in the big '57 Chrysler we rebuilt together. Popeye wasn't even talking to me, which is probably why Dickey wanted to drive me up. My mother looked like she might cry, but she didn't. My father didn't seem to understand. He had convinced himself that in the end I would go into the army because I had to. My brother felt betrayed.

I looked around my parents' house for things from this life that I could bring to my new one. I tried to find my piece of Montana jade but I couldn't. I took my diary, which I hadn't written in since high school. I might need a friend to talk to in Canada.

I've decided to go to Toronto after all, even though the cookies cost more. They have more draft resisters there and more help for them. Toronto seems to be the place to start. They also have a good university with a graduate biology department, recommended by old Professor Moreland at Whiting. He seemed to be about the only person from college who was interested in helping me and he said he could get me into the biology department.

The Chrysler has so much power Dickey has to struggle to keep the speed under ninety. He wears his green combat fatigues from Vietnam, which are not warm enough for Canada. I stick with my World War II fatigues, built for one of the coldest European winters on record and warm enough even for Canada.

I haven't thought about getting driving directions. I figured you just go north and then you're in Canada. But Dickey seems to know where he's going. He drives across the Peace Bridge. This time I cross over to the other side instead of standing on it in protest.

In Toronto at last, I feel sad saying good-bye to Dickey. We hug in our different-colored combat fatigues and I can feel that he is shivering. I go to an address listed in the *Manual for Draft-Age Immigrants to Canada*. There are a lot of people who want to help me here—Unitarians, Episcopalians, Jews, Canadians, Americans. They have a house where you can go for help and information. We all just call it "the House." Down the street from the House is a bar, the Pub, where all the Americans go to drink, listen to music—Jimi Hendrix, Janis Joplin, Country Joe and the Fish—and play darts. I have never played darts before but after a while I start to get good. Some of these Americans at the Pub are draft dodgers like me. Some are veterans. Some, you can't tell why they are here. A few probably work for the FBI, keeping track of their departed citizens.

I am living in a small basement apartment on a nice tree-lined street in Toronto. It was a leafy street when I got here, but not anymore. The dreaded Canadian winter has set in but it doesn't seem any worse than a New England winter—except when the wind is blowing off the lake.

I'm allowed to work, but the only work I can find is through a temporary agency, which sends me one week to an office and the next to a construction site. I am used to this kind of work because, due to my draft status, I did the same sort of temporary work in the U.S. while waiting for my hearings. Once I was even on one of those television shows where they try to catch people looking stupid. I was sent to this office where helium balloons floated to the ceiling and I was supposed to chase them and get all flustered. But I could hear the TV crew behind a partition giving camera instructions and laughing. They seemed to think it was funny that I couldn't get a better job. They never ran the segment on television because I didn't chase the balloons, so it wasn't funny enough.

CHAPTER TWENTY-SEVEN
A NEW LIFE

February 3, 1972

Dear Diary,
*   This idea that I had, that I would be alone, writing my thoughts in a diary, has not turned out to be true. I think this will be my final entry.*
*   Through Professor Morehead I was able to get into a graduate program with Arthur M. Cantwell, one of the leading authorities on wolves in North America. Next summer I will be going on a wolf study program with Cantwell in western Ontario.*

I am excited about the program since Cantwell knows more about wolves than anyone alive. But I am also excited because Hillary Freeman is in the program and going with me for the summer. Hillary is a very fit blond woman who, dressed in blue jeans and flannels, looks like the westerner she is. She comes from the mountains in Alberta. It was clear to me the day I met her that she is also brilliant. I soon realized that everybody in the biology department knew Hillary was brilliant. Hillary does not really care that I am an American draft dodger. She thinks everyone should be a draft dodger and that it is the only sensible position but she doesn't really talk about it very much. What she likes to talk about is wolves. We are both fascinated by their intricate society, how attached they are to the pack, how many rules there are, and how many different roles for different wolves there are within the pack.

To me, wolves are much like the Vietnamese people. Maybe human conflicts are part of the natural order just like Moreland said. Wolves are despised creatures. They are said to be violent and cruel. Ferocious hunters, they work in packs, some hamstringing the legs of the prey while another rips its throat. But they only kill for food or for survival and are otherwise very affectionate animals, closely related to dogs. It is the human beings who kill without reason. They have killed so many wolves in the U.S. that the wolf could face extinction. Humans justify this by telling stories of the vicious wolf—the schoolteacher torn open, the rancher ripped apart, the children dragged away.

In truth, there is not one documented case of a wolf attacking a human in North America. They do not see people as food, so they do not attack them. Why do people keep telling these stories? Of course it is to create an excuse to kill these animals that they do not even like to eat. So the real question is: Why do people kill wolves?

Hillary and I can spend long evenings discussing this round and round—what it means and what it teaches us about ourselves. All of this has great meaning because it gets at the nature of human beings and at the roots of their violence, which is something I want to understand. And having this beautiful and brilliant woman to study with is making me see a pathway to a good life.

I have written my parents about Hillary and my mother is very happy. Just between you and me, Diary, Mom is happy because she confuses the name "Freeman" with "Friedman" and thinks that Hillary is Jewish, which she certainly isn't. Mom keeps asking for a photograph and I don't send one because she would see Hillary's blond, western looks and instantly realize the truth. But I haven't given

Mom *much* to be happy about so I *am* going to let this deception go on just a little longer.

I feel that I have finally found my life and maybe that was the purpose of this journal—and so the diary is ending.

Joel

CHAPTER TWENTY-EIGHT
CAVALRY TO THE RESCUE

Stanley calls me. He is visiting Toronto with three friends. They kept testing his albumen and he kept eating eggs. He says, "Eventually, I would do anything rather than eat one more egg. Even Vietnam sounded better than eating an egg.

"I was in Vietnam for two months, out on patrol, when there was an attack from the side." He points over to his left. We are sitting on stools in the Pub, a peaceful enough place, and it sounds like Stanley talking about our childhood war games. I am thinking he is about to take out the Japanese flag and tell me how he surrendered but instead he pulls on the shoulder of his baggy T-shirt and shows me a shiny round silvery scar the size of a quarter, near the top of his chest.

"Sergeant Boomer, we called him. Swung his piece around to where they were attacking and blew a hole in me instead. Took one for America." He empties the shot glass of whiskey he has in his hand and orders another.

One of his friends who was playing darts comes over. Stanley and his friends are all in civilian clothes except for army T-shirts and they have long hair and don't look at all like soldiers. The friend says, "Stanley was stupid enough to get shot by us. But he's not the stupidest asshole here. Look." He pulls up his shirt and turns his back to me. "Look at that," he says, pointing out a large scar the size of a misshapen saucer on the lower left part of his back. "And then this—through the lung, baby." He turns around and holds up his first two fingers. "Twice, man. Shot both times by friendly Americans. Genuine American friendly fire. But I'm still not the stupidest. See that one over there?" He points at one of the darts players, who throws and then smiles. "He actually got shot by the damned enemy!"

They all laugh. They are drunk and getting drunker. "I mean, it's one thing to get shot by us. Can't help that. But to expose yourself to enemy fire? Man, that's dumb," he shouts.

I am too curious. I have to ask. "Stanley?"

"Yeah, man?"

"You still have the stone?"

He stares at me. Then he smiles. Then he laughs. He is shaking with laughter and his fist is pounding the bar. He struggles to gain control and then says in a hoarse whisper, "I carried that fucking thing everywhere. I even took it to Nam with me. Carried it into fucking battle, man." He is staring at me. "Had it on me when I was wounded. Woke up in the hospital . . ." His voice breaks and he wheezes into laughter. "I woke up and the thing was fucking gone!" Now he is looking angry. "Can you believe it? Someone stole my green stone!"

"Well," I say with a smile, "it *was* jade, you know."

Stanley laughs. "Montana jade, baby!"

One of the darts players starts half singing and half shouting at the music, "And it's one, two, three."

And we all screech back, "What're we fighting for!" It's a great song, but these guys are starting to remind me of how if you smack a lightbulb it will burn brighter. The trouble is, it will burn out that much faster.

"Wait a minute, man!" Stanley bellows. "Hold the game." He starts fumbling through the pockets of his green jacket. "Where the hell is the damn thing?" Then he pulls out a medal dangling from a purple ribbon. I have never seen one before but I know what it is. It is a Purple Heart.

He staggers up to the dartboard and, putting a dart through the purple ribbon, hangs the medal so that the gold-trimmed purple heart with George Washington on it is directly over the bull's-eye.

All four veterans begin furiously throwing darts. One hits the medal but the dart bounces off. "Shit!" Stanley shouts, and he charges the board with a dart in his fist and begins stabbing at the medal. There are tears running down his cheeks. The others grab him and take away the dart. They take down the medal and put it in his pocket and start leading him to the door.

"Hey!" he hollers. "Hey, man!" He is shouting at me. "You know who bought it?"

"Bought it?" I ask, hoping I don't understand, but I do.

"Greased. Wiped out. Dead."

"Who?" I say, dreading the answer.

"Your old buddy." He sways a little as though losing his balance. I am still waiting. "Big Tony Scaratini! Big Tony thought he was tough until he ran up against Charlie."

Charlie. They had this first name for the enemy because the enemy was their friend, someone who could understand them far better than I ever can.

"What happened?" I ask, feeling sick. "What happened to Tony?"

"Don't know. I heard about it just before I was hit.

Somewhere up north. It's a joke, isn't it? That's the end of Big Tony. Remember he never wanted to get killed when we were kids." He does a husky-voiced Tony Scaratini impression, like all us kids used to do. "I'm not dead. I'm keeping da hat." Stanley starts laughing but he could never do a good Scaratini like Donnie LePine. "Or maybe Charlie didn't get him. Maybe we shot him. They're going to kill us all. Cavalry to the rescue. Yes sir. Air Cav will kill us all—'cause we're air mobile!"

I don't really know what he is saying but then he starts crying again and the others lead him away.

CHAPTER TWENTY-NINE
JUST LIKE THAT

Just like that. Tony Scaratini's life is over. I have not been in a very good frame of mind since Stanley's visit. Now I am going over to the House to see if I can find out what happened to Tony Scaratini. But Hillary stops me as I am leaving to tell me she is not going on the Ontario wolf project this summer. The U.S. government has a new project to introduce Canadian wolves to parts of Idaho and Montana where the local hunters and ranchers have killed off the population. It is an exciting and controversial project because, of course, the people who killed all the American wolves will want to kill the Canadian ones too, saying that they are killing sheep and threatening children and could destroy the ranching industry—just like the Vietnamese are spreading Communism and endangering our way of life. But this time the federal government is going to protect the wolves. I envy Hillary working on this but we both know I won't be able to go because it involves traveling in the U.S. She says she will be back in six months but for some reason I don't think she will.

So now, on my way to find out about Tony Scaratini, I have more than one reason to be in a dark mood. The House has information on everything about the war. You can even find out how many Purple Hearts they have given in Vietnam. So far it's almost two hundred thousand. Almost fifty thousand American troops have been killed. They warn you that the number changes every day. There may be a few more since I read the number a few minutes ago.

The House doesn't tell you how many Vietnamese have been killed. The U.S. military does. They call it the "body count." The body count is a tricky thing. They like to give the body count because it shows that a lot more of them are dying than us. It makes it look like we're winning. But we're not. On the other hand, they don't want too high a body count. They don't like to count the civilians and they like to keep the Vietnamese casualty number down—far ahead of ours but not so high that people can see what a slaughter the whole thing is.

The House has a book, really a stack of papers two inches thick, bound with rings, listing everyone killed in Vietnam. It gives last name first and then "KIA," killed in action. I turn to "S" to look for "Scaratini, Anthony." There is Sabatini . . . Scaller, Scanlon, Scranton . . ." I stop and think a second. Scranton. "Scr" is after "Scar." Scaratini isn't there. I go back and check again. Could they have misspelled his name? I check every name under "S," all six pages, and Tony is not there. It's not true. He wasn't killed. But there is something hypnotic about leafing through these names of the dead, as though by looking at their names I am acknowledging their deaths and in that way giving them life. There are so many of them. So many names. Imagine this many bodies. I look for LePine but there isn't one. I wonder if he ever did volunteer. I haven't heard from him. What about Lester? I turn to "P" for Parkman. Parker, Parks . . . no Parkman. Lester made it. He probably has his high school job back in Indiana by now. And then—

It is as though something has slapped me in the face. No, not slapped. Punched, sharp and hard, and I feel sick to my stomach and a little dizzy. I look again. I have not imagined it.

Pizzutti, Rocco.

Had Myron been wrong? Or did Rocco just decide to volunteer? Oh, Rocco. What a waste. What an unbelievable waste. I think of Angela, who has now lost a father and a brother to war. There is a kind of librarian in charge of all these papers, a tall woman with long straight blond hair, a face with no trace of humor; she wears round wire-rimmed glasses like John Lennon.

I ask her if there are any records of who was a draftee and who was a volunteer. She says that there aren't, that they have no records on the dead whatsoever—unless they got a medal. They do have medal citations. "He's dead," I say. "Do they give dead people medals?"

The humorless woman almost smiles. "They give most of the medals to dead people," she says, and she hands me another ring-bound pile even thicker than the list of the dead. Much thicker. In fact, there are two of them. I take M–Z.

There it is. Pizzutti, Rocco (KIA).

Rocco got a Silver Star and a Purple Heart. He was a "war hero." How he would have hated that. Suddenly I understand Stanley and why he hates his medal. I want to take that Silver Star and that Purple Heart, the two seedy little baubles that are supposed to replace Rocco. I want to stab them with darts just like Stanley did. I want to deface them. Instead, because it is all I can do, I read on.

PIZZUTTI, ROCCO (KIA), Citation:
The President of the United States
takes pride in presenting the
Silver Star Medal (posthumously) to
Rocco Pizzutti, Specialist Fourth
Class, U.S. Army, for gallantry in
action while engaged in military
operations against an armed hostile
force in the Republic of Vietnam.
Specialist Four Pizzutti
distinguished himself while serving
as a Rifleman with Company A, 3rd
Battalion, 12th Infantry Regiment,
4th Infantry Division. On 1 July
1969, Specialist Pizzutti was on
one of the first helicopters to set
down in a landing zone northwest of
Kon Tum and immediately assumed a
position to provide security for
the incoming helicopters. As the
third helicopter touched down, an
unknown-sized enemy force subjected
the landing zone with intense
automatic weapons, small arms, and
mortar fire. A hand grenade landed

```
one meter from Specialist Pizzutti
at the feet of an officer and three
other enlisted men. Without
hesitating and with remarkable
athleticism, Specialist Pizzutti
ran to the grenade, scooped it up,
and . . .
```

I'm not reading on. I know what happened. Rocco always had complete faith in his athletic ability. He thought that with his powerful left arm he could throw the grenade in time, but it was too late. I don't want to read how badly he got it, whether it was instant, or how many men he saved. He is dead. What else is there? All fifty thousand of them have their stories. The Detroit Tigers lost a great left-handed pitcher. Who knows what else was lost with these fifty thousand men? When is this going to stop? Rocco. This was not Rocco's destiny. Of all of us, Rocco was the one who seemed destined for better things. Most people thought it was Donnie but I always thought Rocco was the one with a destiny. And this wasn't it.

CHAPTER THIRTY
ROCCO'S DESTINY

I want to talk to Angela but this is the only phone number I can find. "Hello, Mrs. Pizzutti." I did not really know her. She seemed an angry woman, a little scary when we were kids, and Rocco and Angela didn't bring us around to their house. "Hello, Mrs. Pizzutti, it's Joel Bloom."

"Joel Blo—from Canada, I suppose."

"That's right. I just heard about Rocco."

"Did you? So the news has finally reached the safety of Canada."

"I'm sorry, Mrs. Pizzutti. I just heard." I don't know

what to say, so I say what I am feeling. "I feel sick, Mrs. Pizzutti. I loved Rocco. I always thought that he was the best
of us."

"He was. He was." I can tell by her voice that this has
softened her a little. "You know, Joel, he got two medals."

"Yes, I heard."

"A Silver Star and a Purple Heart. His father also got a
Purple Heart. I have them on the wall right next to each
other. But Rocco got the Silver Star too."

"Yes, he was a hero," I hear myself say. I know this is
the kind of lie that keeps wars going, but now I also understand that this way of talking was invented because there is
nothing else you can say to all the Mrs. Pizzuttis. I ask for
Angela but she says she doesn't live there anymore and
gives me another phone number.

X X X

"Hello, Angela?"

"Joel!"

"How did you know it was me?"

"I knew you would call when you heard."

"How'd you know?"

"Rocco always said it."

"What?"

"Never mind. He talked about you a lot. So did I. When he got drafted I kept telling him to go to Canada and join Joel Bloom."

"But he wouldn't do it."

"He just said that Major League Baseball wasn't in Canada."

"Yeah, he loved baseball."

"Yeah, he loved it so much he was willing to kill Vietnamese people just so he could play." Her voice was turning to that husky angry tone she used to have when she talked about the Kennedy assassination. "I think baseball and the military work hand in hand. They were the ones . . ."

I am not really listening. I'm thinking about Rocco, about how he could never bring himself to hurt a frog. I ask where she is living and she says, "Roxbury. I'm a social worker."

"That's great," I say, and start thinking about how in my generation it will be the women who do all the interesting things while the men get drafted.

"It's not that great. Hasn't worked out like I thought it would. Can I come see you?"

✕ ✕ ✕

I was expecting her. There was a doorbell ringing. I opened the door and she was standing on the stoop holding a suitcase, her black eyes burning through the icy air, and we both knew that she was never leaving.

It is funny the way when you see adults you knew as a kid, they look different. Angela had the same fiery black eyes and thick black hair on the verge of flying wild. But though she looked the same as she always had, I now realized that she didn't really look at all like Rocco. In fact, she was stunning—thrillingly beautiful. How was it that I had never noticed this before?

She said that even after I moved to Canada, Rocco was always certain we would get together. "Rocco was like that," she said. "He never doubted things. He knew he would make the major leagues. He was certain he wouldn't get hurt in Vietnam."

✕ ✕ ✕

I am pretty much a Canadian now. There are rumors that Major League Baseball is going to expand, start new teams everywhere. Some people say there might even be one here in Toronto.

I heard that Rachel Apfelbaum married Donnie LePine. I never saw that coming. Then they went to law school together. I got one letter from Donnie but it didn't say anything about Rachel. He did say that he had tried to volunteer for the army but they wouldn't take him—"saw through my plan," he said. I never hear from them. Maybe they're embarrassed. Your best friend isn't supposed to marry your girlfriend, even your ex-girlfriend. But it doesn't matter to me. It all seems far away.

Stanley has come up here two other times for visits. He doesn't seem any better. I hear from Dickey every once in a while. But I have my own life here and Haley seems a very long time ago.

Looking at the whole thing, I have to say that I'm proud that I wasn't the German. That I took my stand and never hurt anyone. Except the time I punched Scaratini. I still feel bad about that.

But at least he was the only person I ever hurt. I have never killed any Vietnamese people. I feel good about that. I have never killed a German or a Japanese or a Korean. The day before Martin Luther King Jr. was killed, he talked about how people who didn't stand up for anything were dead though they didn't know it. I didn't understand that at the time. But now I do.

I suppose I did hurt my family and I don't feel good about that. I don't have much contact with Sam. I am not sure if he is angry or if he just does not want to be seen having a connection to me. He did get a job with the McGovern campaign, one of the most catastrophic presidential runs in

American history. McGovern campaigned against the war and only Massachusetts and Washington DC voted for him. Maybe Sam helped them carry Massachusetts. McGovern lost to Nixon, a man almost nobody likes, who kept insisting that if we bombed enough villages the Vietnamese would surrender. His campaign was caught burglarizing the Democratic Party offices.

Still, everyone voted for him. And the war goes on.

My parents write to me and my mother keeps sending Hebrew National salamis. She seems to think that I am lost on frozen tundra without salamis. So I am glad that they are coming to visit and can see what a good city Toronto is.

My mother brings me a box of salamis. I show them around Toronto—the theaters, the music, the lakefront. I show my mother that there are a lot of Jewish people in Toronto and a lot of Jewish food—much more than in Haley.

They are somber, as though a great tragedy has befallen me. I try to show them that I am all right. Someday someone of my generation will become president and we will all be pardoned. But I probably will never go back. Just because America forgives me does not mean I have to forgive America. Angela says she wishes she had left right after John Kennedy was killed.

Before my parents leave my father says to me in the same

voice he used to use down in the shelter with the canned tuna, "I'm sorry you've had to go through all this."

But I'm not sorry at all. How often do you get a chance to stand for something? Refusing to go to war was actually one of the best moments of my life.

Angela and I don't stay in Toronto. We move to Alberta to work with wolves that raise families and build communities in the pine forests, prowling the blue-rock snow-capped mountains killing elk, deer, and moose for the survival of their pack. But they treat their fellow wolves with love and the greatest respect. Sometimes they are suspicious of a wolf from another pack. But wolf packs don't go to war with each other. Angela loves the wolves, loves their society, and claims she is still a social worker of a kind. We try to understand them. Sometimes we befriend them.

We are not going to forget or get over anything that happened. But for now we are tired of it all—tired of war and of trying to end it—just fatigued. And in protecting the wolves, misunderstood creatures struggling to survive in their violent but loving world, we begin to understand our world. Angela and I feel that we have been surrounded by war all our lives. Even now, far beyond the high crests of the Canadian Rockies, there is still war. But here we have found peace together. I think Rocco would have liked that.

ACKNOWLEDGMENTS

Thanks to my agent, Charlotte Sheedy, one of those "draft counselors" I wrote about; and to my good friend and publisher, George Gibson, who is the smartest baseball fan I know; and to Nancy Miller, who at last count has edited seventeen of my books—isn't that some kind of record? Also my thanks to Emily Easton, Mary Kate Castellani, and all the people at Bloomsbury and Walker who have taken such painstaking care with this book. Thanks to Marian and Talia for understanding my unpopular ideas.

Also to the memory of John F. Kennedy, Robert F.

Kennedy, Martin Luther King Jr., and more than a dozen other civil rights workers, millions of Vietnamese, and 58,267 Americans whose violent deaths filled my youth with a sadness from which I can never recover, a sadness that gives a wisdom that is at the heart of this book.